PRAISE FOR *I am REBEL*

"A tail-thumping, tongue-lolling treat
full of adventure, humour and heart."
Ross Welford

"*I Am Rebel* both broke my heart and made it sing.
This book is as close to perfect as it's possible to get."
Natasha Farrant

"A beautifully crafted and heartwarming story."
Abi Elphinstone

"An instant classic. Outstanding writing
and a richly adventurous story."
Katya Balen

"A fantastic quest novel that sits between *Charlotte's
Web* and *War Horse*. Rebel's voice is true and clear:
he is the best of dogs and this is the best of books."
Phil Earle

"A beautiful, heartfelt adventure."
Sophie Anderson

"The goodest story about the goodest boy.
I love Rebel like my own dog."
Carlie Sorosiak

ROSS MONTGOMERY

WALKER
BOOKS

First published 2024 by Walker Books Ltd
87 Vauxhall Walk, London SE11 5HJ

2 4 6 8 10 9 7 5 3 1

Text © 2024 Ross Montgomery
Cover illustration © 2024 Keith Robinson

The right of Ross Montgomery to be identified as author
of this work has been asserted in accordance with the
Copyright, Designs and Patents Act 1988

EU Authorized Representative: HackettFlynn Ltd,
36 Cloch Choirneal, Balrothery, Co. Dublin,
K32 C942, Ireland. EU@walkerpublishinggroup.com

This book has been typeset in Adobe Garamond Pro
with Painting With Chocolate and Scarlet Wood

Printed and bound by CPI Group (UK) Ltd, Croydon CR0 4YY

British Library Cataloguing in Publication Data:
a catalogue record for this book is available from the British Library

ISBN 978-1-5295-2995-1

www.walker.co.uk

MIX
Paper | Supporting
responsible forestry
FSC® C171272

"You become responsible,
forever, for what
you have tamed."

The Little Prince
Antoine de Saint-Exupéry

THE LAST PERFECT DAY

1

HOME

The day begins exactly as it should.

It's summer, and dawn is poking its nose through the curtains. Our bed is still warm with the night of sleeping. I can hear a cockerel crowing outside in the farmyard. I can smell bacon downstairs, and hear the clatter of pans on the stove, and Tom's mum and dad talking to each other in soft sleepy voices.

I know, from the moment I wake up, that today is going to be perfect.

Tom is still snoring beside me. I stand up, shake out the last dregs of sleep, and snuffle over to him. He always smells most like himself in the morning: groggy and warm and sleep-drunk, all of him Tom.

That's my first job of the day: wake Tom up. I do it

by licking his face. I love licking his face. It's the best bit of the day.

"Ugh!" Tom groans. "*Yuk,* Rebel."

That's me. I am Rebel. It's the name Tom gave me. He wipes the slobber off his face and hugs me close to him. I love it when he does that.

"Silly old dog," he mumbles.

At this point, I should probably mention that I'm a dog.

But I'm *not* an old dog; I'm only five. And I'm not silly, either. I am a good dog. I know this, because Tom tells me I am good all the time, and Tom knows everything.

Anyway, we can't stay in bed like this. We have so many things to do! Usually I wait for Tom before I go anywhere, but the bacon smell means there might be some rind going spare in the kitchen, and I think it's important for me to find out. I jump off the bed and run downstairs and skitter across the tiles.

There's Dad, sat at the table and already dressed for work on the farm. I sniff his clothes as I run past, all rich with the smell of sheep's wool and sour milk and mud. I like that smell. Mum is hard at work by the stove, wiping her hands on her apron and shifting a big copper kettle. She smells of tea and soap and potatoes and porridge and mutton and gravy, all mixed together. I like that smell even more.

"Ach! Rebel!" Mum tuts, shooing me away. "Take this and leave me alone, will you?"

She picks something out of the pan and tosses it on the floor. Bacon rind! *Yes yes yes yes yes*. I snaffle it straight off the tiles, smoky-rich and succulent, crackling with fat and hot enough to singe the tongue.

I was right. I knew that today was going to be perfect.

Tom comes downstairs, rubbing sleep from his eyes. We sit in the happy fug of the kitchen and eat in silence until the day can begin proper. I'm not allowed to beg at the table, but if I hide under Tom's chair, he secretly feeds me scraps of his breakfast without Mum and Dad noticing. It's the best bit of the day.

"Thank you for doing this," I tell him. "I love you."

Tom doesn't understand me when I talk. He thinks I'm just barking or growling. But on a deeper level, I think he knows what I'm saying. It's like how I can tell that he loves me when he scratches my head or pats my sides or smiles at me. It's always been like that. We've never needed words.

The cockerel crows again, and Dad gets to his feet. "Right! Come on, lad. Let's not let the best of the day get ahead of us."

Dad says that every morning. "All right, all right," sighs Tom. He says *that* every morning, too.

He shovels down the rest of his breakfast, and we race outside together. And there it all is, in one big, beautiful moment: the sunrise over the fields, the first smells of the farmyard, the first fingertips of wind across the mountains, the whole length of a day spread out before us.

It's wrong, what I said before. *That's* the best bit of the day: the first moment I see the farm, and remember how lucky I am to be here.

I love the farm. I've lived on it every day of my life, ever since Tom found me as a puppy and brought me home to live with him. I've never left it, not once. I've never even been through the front gate.

Every day on the farm is the same as the one before it. First, we go to Bottom Field and see how the sheep are doing. Tom and Mum and Dad are sheep farmers. Tom says that around here, everyone keeps sheep. People make clothes from sheep's wool and sell sheep's milk and cheese to get by. It's got harder to do that over the last few years, because of all the taxes that the King keeps collecting. Tom and Dad get milking and shearing while I bound around and see how everyone is doing.

"Morning, Agnes! How's the hoof, Beth? Looking good, Kitty!"

"Hungry," the sheep reply. "Hungry, hungry, hungry."

That's as far as the conversation goes. The sheep don't have very much to say for themselves, but I'm happy to chat anyway. It doesn't cost anything to be polite.

I know I'm not much of a sheepdog. I'm small and I've got stumpy legs and I can't run very fast and my bark isn't scary. Dad always says that he wishes Tom had found himself a *proper* farm dog instead of a scruffy old stray like me, but I know he doesn't really mean it, because whenever no one's looking, he scrunches me behind the ears and whispers that I'm the best dog in the whole wide world.

Bottom Field is where I usually find Priscilla, dozing under a tree. Priscilla is the farm cat. She's not allowed to go in the house – if she does, Mum chases her out with a poker – so she's lived outside her whole life. She smells like dust and old flowers.

"Morning, Priscilla!" I say cheerfully.

"Go away," she mutters.

Priscilla is always like this. "Nice day for it," I say.

She opens up a yellow eye and glares at me. "What's nice about it?"

I have to stop and think about that. "Everything?"

"Rebel! Come on!" Tom shouts behind me.

Tom needs me! I'm a good dog, so I always come when he calls. I start running away and Priscilla gives me a knowing laugh. "Yes, off you go, farm dog. Your master's waiting."

I stop. I hate it when she says that. "Tom's not my *master*."

"Really? Then how come you do everything he says?" Priscilla sighs and stretches lazily. "Poor old Rebel. Not much going on upstairs, is there?"

Ha! Priscilla is so stupid sometimes. There aren't any stairs in the field! I dart after Tom, laughing all the way.

After the milking and shearing is done, Mum brings us lunch. Actually it's just for Dad and Tom, because dogs don't have lunch. I know this, because they keep telling me to stop begging and leave them alone. Lunch is always chunks of cold pie and fresh apples and sour sheep's cheese and it smells so good. Tom will wait until Dad isn't looking and then toss me some so that I can eat it. He's always thinking of me. He is so clever. I love him so much.

After lunch, we move the sheep from Bottom Field up to Top Field, because that's where the best grass is. Tom's job is to stay with them until sunset to make sure they don't escape, or get stolen by thieves, or eaten by wolves. I stay with him, even though I'm frightened of wolves, because that's my job. Wherever Tom goes, I go too. I'm his dog and he's my boy. I would die for him if I had to.

Soon Dad heads back to the farm, and that's it. It's just me and Tom and the sheep now for *hours*. We can do whatever we want! First, I find a stick and drag it over for him to throw.

Tom sighs. "Rebel, why do you always have to choose the biggest stick you can find?"

"Uush hhrrow ihh," I mumble through a mouthful of stick.

"Get a smaller one."

I do as he says, because I'm a good dog. Tom picks up the stick.

"You want me to throw it?"

"Yes, please," I say eagerly.

"This stick here?" he asks with a grin, waving it. "Really?"

My tail wags furiously. I love it when he does this. "Yes, throw it now, please."

"Are you sure?"

This is so good. "Yes!"

"All right, all right, stop barking."

Tom throws it and I bring it back, and we do that over and over again. Sometimes Tom chases me, and sometimes I chase him. Sometimes I'll run around on my own barking, because I'm happy and it feels so good to run, but mainly because it makes Tom laugh, and it's the best sound in the whole world. Afterwards I lie on my back so Tom can scratch my tummy. I love it when he does that.

"Little Belly," he says fondly.

That's his special name for me. It's a bit like Rebel, but it's also about my tummy. Tom came up with that. He is so clever.

Me and Tom, just the two of us. Now *that's* the best bit of the day. I mean it this time.

After that, we settle down until evening. By now, the sun is sinking over the mountains, ripening the sky in reds and purples. You can see the whole entire world from Top Field: all the other houses and farms, stretching right up to the mountains.

Tom pulls out a sketchpad and charcoal from his knapsack and starts drawing. He loves drawing – his pad and charcoal go everywhere with him. I lean against his chest and drink in his warmth while he smudges out a new picture.

"See, Rebel? It's you and me, climbing that mountain."

Tom always draws me and him together. That's the way it's meant to be. He talks as he draws, the words coming as easily as the lines come out on the paper. He's happiest when he draws, even more Tom than when he's asleep.

"They say there's a waterfall on the other side of that mountain, even bigger than the one in Brennock. They say wild flowers grow either side of it, like a carpet, stretching to the sea. Daisies all the way down! Can you imagine that, Rebel?"

I *can't* imagine it. I've never seen a waterfall, or the sea. I've never left the farm. I don't even know what a carpet is.

Tom has never seen the sea, either: the furthest he's ever gone is the market in Connick. He always talks about the different places he'll visit one day, but I don't think he means it. Why would he leave when everything we need is right here?

Then Tom stops drawing. It takes me a moment to realize that he's seen something.

Through the trees in the distance, you can see a little stretch of the road to Connick. There are two men walking down it. They're both wearing golden jackets, and they both have shiny black boots and shiny black belts. They're both carrying muskets.

It's the King's guardsmen. You often see them patrolling the roads in twos or threes like this. Tom once told me that they're checking that everyone on the road has a permit. He said that if you don't pay the King's taxes on time, the guardsmen take away your permit, which means you can't use the roads, which means you can't sell at market, which means you make no money, which means no bacon at breakfast.

That's not all the guardsmen do. They make sure that no one ever leaves their home at night. They make sure no one says anything against the King, either. If they find out you've been bad-mouthing him, they take you away and you don't come back. I've heard Mum and Dad talking about it in hushed voices when Tom's not in the room.

Mum and Dad say that it didn't use to be like this. Before the King, folk could say whatever they wanted. But then the King took over and decided that he needed everything for himself. There were people who tried to fight back, called the Reds, but they were no match for the guardsmen and their guns and they all got taken away. So now no one fights back, and the guardsmen patrol the roads, and that's just how it is.

I hear a sharp brittle *snap* beside me, like a tiny bone being broken. Tom has gripped his charcoal so hard that it's crumbled to ash and smeared black powder all over his lovely picture.

"Aw, heck," he mutters crossly.

"Tom! Dinner!"

I hear Mum before Tom does, because my ears are better than his. I run around and bark because this is very, very important.

"All right, all right!" he murmurs. "Calm down, Rebel."

I can't be calm. I *won't* be calm. Our work is over. Now the best bit of the day – the *real* best bit – can begin.

Tom gathers up the flock and drives them back down to Bottom Field. I charge ahead, my nose raised until I find the scent I'm looking for. And there it is, weaving out of the chimney like a golden ribbon and twisting across the fields towards me.

Stew. Lamb stew: deep, glossy, rich, lamb stew, simmering on the stove with a skin on top. Lamb stew with carrots and gravy, ladled into thick stone bowls. Lamb stew means lamb bones. Lamb bones mean bone marrow. And bone marrow means amazing, delicious dinner for good dogs like Rebel.

I was right all along. Today is absolutely perfect.

By the time Tom catches up with me, I'm already scratching at the farmhouse door and whining. He pushes it open and I scramble inside. The kitchen is golden and glowing with the smell of lamb. I run to my bowl and there it is! A lamb bone plucked straight from the pot, curling with steam and glistening with blobs of fat. I'm so happy I spin in circles and lick every inch of the bone. Stew, stew, stew, stew, *stew*!

"Stew again, is it?" says Tom with a sigh as he slumps into his chair.

"Hush," chides Mum, hitting him lightly with a spoon. "You're lucky we have anything. There's plenty around here that don't."

"I know," Tom murmurs quietly.

"Guardsmen were on the road tonight," says Dad, eating cheerfully.

Mum shrugs. "They're always on the road."

"But never *this* often. Not so many. Not around here, so far from the High Castle." Dad scrapes his bowl with his spoon. "Something important must be happening."

"That'd make a change," mutters Tom.

"Eat your stew," snaps Mum.

Once dinner is over, that's us done for the day. I scamper upstairs before Tom, so I can warm the bed for him. That's another of my very important jobs. Tom follows more slowly and takes off his work clothes before flopping into bed beside me. He doesn't blow out his candle straight away like he normally does. Instead he just stares at the ceiling.

"Daisies all the way down," he sighs.

He's thinking about sad things again. He's doing that a lot nowadays. I snuffle closer to him so he knows I'm here, and that I'll *always* be here, because I'm his dog and he's my boy and I love him. He places his hand on my back, and the soft weight of his palm is the most perfect weight there is.

When Tom's breathing becomes slow and steady and his body sinks soft in the bed, I know that my day is finally done and I can go to sleep like a good dog.

I was wrong all the other times. *That's* the best moment of the day: me and Tom, back in the blankets, safe and warm, knowing that today has been kind to us and tomorrow will be just as good. That we have everything we need, and we always will, because nothing on the farm will ever change.

Why would it change, when it's already so perfect?

THE
DAY IT
CHANGES

2
INTRUDERS

I know that everything is wrong from the moment I open my eyes. Someone is shouting downstairs. A man. "I *said* you don't have a choice!"

I jump off the bed and scramble downstairs as fast as I can. I don't recognize the voice. That means there's a stranger in the house. I have to get rid of them. I have to protect Tom.

When I get downstairs, Dad is standing beside the table with his hat in his hands, looking small and frightened. Mum is pressed into the corner of the kitchen, glaring at the intruders in her home.

There are two of them. One is standing blocking the doorway; the other is leaning back in Dad's chair, his muddy boots on the table and his musket resting in his lap. They're both wearing jackets made of gold thread.

Guardsmen!

I sense right away that they're dangerous. The one in the doorway looks like a slug – the one in the chair looks like a rat. They both smell mean, and wrong, and bad. I know what guns can do. I've seen Dad kill rabbits just by pointing the barrel and pulling the trigger. I growl at the men and Rat whips around in the chair, fixing me with his mean little rat eyes.

"Get that dog out of here!" he snaps.

Dad nods quickly. "Yes, sir. Right away, sir." He tries to drag me back by the scruff of the neck, but I keep growling and pulling against him. I can't let Dad take me away. I have to get the danger out!

"Rebel, no!"

Tom bursts into the kitchen behind me and scoops me up in his arms. He glances around, confused. "What's going on?"

Mum points at the intruders. "They want more taxes – *that's* what's going on!"

Tom grows pale. "But we've already paid for this month. And the next."

"Not any more, you haven't," says Slug with a smirk. "New orders from the King. Double taxes."

Tom splutters in shock. "We don't have that kind of money. No one does!"

The two guardsmen chuckle.

"Tough luck, sonny," says Rat. "No taxes, no road permit. Starve, if that's what you want."

I can feel Tom squeezing me tighter as he grows angrier. "You can't do that!"

Dad stops him with a wave of his hand. "We'll pay up – just give us a few more days."

"Glad to hear it." Rat stands up and shoulders his musket. "And while we're here, we're looking for a man in a wolfskin. He's been spotted in the area. He's dangerous – a troublemaker. Wanted by the King himself. Anyone found harbouring him will be shot on sight."

No one has anything to say to that. Rat nods curtly to Slug, and they turn to leave, the squeak of their polished leather boots cutting through the silence.

"We'll be back at the end of the week," says Rat over his shoulder. "Make sure you have the money. The last farmer that refused had his house torched and his fields salted."

He's halfway out of the door when Tom finds his voice again.

"You won't keep getting away with this!" he cries. "Sooner or later, people are going to make the King pay for what he's done, and then you'll be sorry!"

The room freezes, like a startled cat. Nobody moves. Then the guardsmen both turn to face Tom.

"What did you just say?" Slug's voice uncurls like an eel from a cave.

"Sounded like Red talk to me," says Rat. "You a Red, boy? Calling your dog Rebel and talking treason?"

I have no idea what Rat means – I didn't know that "Rebel" meant anything bad.

Dad jumps in front of Tom, panicking. "No! He's just a stupid boy – a kid."

Rat shoves Dad aside and leans in close to Tom. I can smell the menace thrumming from him like a hot iron. I'm terrified, but I have to be brave. I have to protect Tom! I bark and bare my teeth, but the guardsman just keeps staring at Tom.

"How old are you, boy? Sixteen?"

People always think Tom's older than he is. Mum says he's tall for his age.

"T-twelve," he whispers.

Rat smirks. "You know what we did to the last Red we caught? Shooting him would have been a mercy, boy. Think you're old enough for that, do you?"

Tom shakes his head. Rat nods to Slug, and a wordless message seems to pass through the air between them, because Slug instantly walks to the crockery cabinet and raises the butt of his musket.

"No!" Mum cries.

Slug brings the musket down and smashes all the plates inside the cabinet, every single one. Dad rushes to Mum, holding her back while she clenches her fists and tears run silently down her face. Rat doesn't take his eyes off Tom the entire time. When it's done, he turns and strides out of the kitchen, crunching shards of broken crockery beneath his boots.

"End of the week," he repeats, "or the tax is tripled."

Slug spits on the floor and then follows him out of the farmhouse.

Tom finally releases me and I tear after the guardsmen, barking at their backs as they stalk out of the farm. I can't believe what has just happened – I'm shaking all over with fear, from my head to the tip of my tail. I didn't protect Tom when I should have done, but I can protect him now. I have to make sure that the guardsmen never come back. I bark and bark at them, but they don't even falter. They just keep strolling away, as if they have all the time in the world. My voice sounds small and hollow as it echoes through the farmyard.

3
THE REDS

By the time I get back to the kitchen, Tom and Mum and Dad are already shouting at one another.

"What do you think you were doing?" Dad roars at Tom. "Talking like that to the King's guard? Are you trying to get arrested?"

Tom's face burns with anger. "What are *you* doing, calling them *sir*? Double taxes? There's no way we can pay that! You *know* we don't have the money!"

Dad swallows. "It's fine. We'll take extra sheep to the market at Connick this week..."

"Who's going to buy them now?" Mum scoffs. "Everyone's in the same boat as us – no one'll have any money!"

Dad rubs his face and sits down heavily. I've never

seen him look so tired or miserable. "Then we'll go further – the big market at Unsk, maybe. They'll still have money there."

"You'll never get back before the curfew starts," snaps Mum. "You know the rule – anyone outside after sundown gets arrested!"

Dad grits his teeth in frustration. "What else can we do?"

Tom rests his hands firmly on the table. "There *is* something we can do, Dad. We can refuse. We can refuse to pay the new taxes."

His breathing is rapid, like he's finally letting out all the anger and frustration that's been held inside him for months.

"It's all folk at the market have been talking about. People have started saying they won't pay. They're standing against the guardsmen all over the country, and saying they won't put up with it any more!"

Dad stares at him. "Who's been filling your head with this rubbish? Was it Old Laurie? Oh, when I get my hands on him…"

Tom doesn't back down. His eyes are gleaming

with excitement. "Don't you see? We could do it here! If every farm in the area refused to pay, there's no way the guardsmen could arrest us all!"

"But they could string you up from the trees before the week is out!" Mum cries. "Is *that* what you want, Tom?"

She sinks down into a chair. When she next speaks, her voice comes out small and sad, like soft rain against the windows.

"You were too little to remember the first time the Reds fought back against the King. But we do, Tom. We saw what happens to people with big ideas who think they can change the world."

"But it's different this time, Mum," Tom argues excitedly. "Back then, the Reds were spread out all over the country. If we *all* fought back at the same time—"

"Enough!" Dad suddenly shouts, slamming his fist on the table.

I've never heard Dad shout like that before. I've never seen him so angry. I hide under the table and whine.

"A handful of shepherds with red rags tied round their necks aren't going to win a war against *the King*,

Tom!" he bellows. "He has a whole army, with guns and cannons. Better weapons and better training. It's how the Reds were beaten in the first place. These new idiots are going to do nothing except get us all killed!"

"But—" Tom begins.

"*No,*" says Dad. "We're farmers, not fighters. We keep our heads down, and we face what's given to us." He stands up angrily. "Now come on. There's sheep that need looking after."

And with that, he leaves. Tom stays locked in place, shaking as if slapped. Mum wipes her eyes, and kneels down to gather up the broken plates from the floor in silence.

There is no bacon.

The rest of the day is miserable. The sky is glum and heavy with clouds, and Tom and Dad won't speak to each other. Dad keeps his head bowed and Tom keeps his mouth clenched. Once the sheep are up in Top Field, Dad storms back to the house and Tom sinks to the ground like he's been carrying big heavy rocks all day.

It's all up to me now. I have to cheer Tom up. I have to show him that underneath it all, things are still OK.

There might be clouds in the sky, but the sun's always shining behind them.

I bring him a stick, but Tom doesn't want to throw it. I try running around and barking, but *that* doesn't work, either. He isn't even drawing like he usually does. He's just staring out across the mountains in silence.

There's only one thing for it. I sit down and lean against him, so he knows he's not alone. That I'm here, and I love him. And sure enough, it works. It always does. He rests his hand against me and I feel him relax for the first time that day.

"It's not right, Rebel," says Tom quietly. "This is *our* land. We can't let the King take it from us just because he wants to." He points ahead. "You see that mountain?"

Of course I can. It's the biggest mountain you can see from Top Field, the very last thing the sun touches.

"The High Castle is on the other side of that mountain," says Tom. "That's where the King lives. They say everything inside is made of gold. They say you could sell a tenth of it and it would feed the country for a whole year, but the King keeps it all for himself."

I can feel him getting angrier and angrier as he

talks. He grabs his charcoal and pad and starts drawing in swift, furious jerks across the paper.

"I've seen pictures of it," says Tom. "It sits at the end of a long, deep gorge. It's got five towers, and the King's flag flies from the tallest one."

It's a good sketch. They always are. The High Castle is broad and strong, filling the end of the gorge like a cork in a bottle. But Tom doesn't stop there.

"Old Laurie says that one day, the Reds will rise up again." His eyes burn as he draws. "Men and women and children from all over the country will come together and throw the King out of the High Castle, once and for all."

I like Old Laurie – when he comes by the house, he always has something tasty in his pocket for me. But I didn't know he was saying stuff like this to Tom. Mum and Dad are right – Tom could get in big trouble for talking like this. He keeps sketching, filling the gorge with thousands of people holding sticks and pitchforks. It's the best drawing he's ever done.

"When the Reds win, Old Laurie says that they'll fly a red flag from the top of the tallest tower. Then everyone will know that the King has gone and his army is defeated and the country is ours once more."

Tom draws himself standing on top of the tallest tower, waving a red flag to the cheering crowds. He draws me standing next to him, just like he always does. Then he stops drawing, and gazes out across the mountains.

"And then we'll be free," he says, his voice almost a whisper. "We'll be able to go wherever we want, and no one will stop us. We'll never have to pay taxes or go hungry or bow to anyone ever aga—"

"That's quite a drawing you have there."

We spin around in shock.

There's a man leaning over the fence behind us, at the point where the field becomes forest. The trees behind him are deep and dark. He has a scar over his left eye, and a dusting of white stubble. His skin is as rough and worn as an old oak.

And his whole body – from head to tail – is covered in the pelt of a wolf.

4
RIDER

*T*he stranger in the wolfskin looks like no one I've ever seen in my life. He looks like he's spent years sleeping in rainstorms and on bare rock. I should have smelled him earlier, but the stranger was clever – he came from downwind. He smells like oil, and leather, and iron, and blood.

I leap to my paws, barking and growling. It's the man Slug and Rat warned us about – the one they said was dangerous. I can't make the same mistake twice. I have to protect Tom!

The man chuckles. "Quite the guard dog you've got there. You wouldn't think it, looking at him."

Rude. I keep barking. Tom is trying to look brave, but I can feel how frightened he is. "Th-that's right. His name's Rebel. He attacks on command."

This is not true. I bit a sheep once, but that was an accident. Tom is lying to make the man go away.

The man doesn't leave; instead he nods approvingly.

"Rebel – a fine name. And you've taught him loyalty too. Worth more than all the gold in the world, that is." He holds out a hand. "How about you, boy? What's your name?"

Tom doesn't take his hand. "You – you shouldn't be here," he stammers. "The guardsmen are looking for you. You need to leave."

The man keeps his hand out for a moment longer, and then drops it.

"Forgive me," he says. "I can see I've startled you, sneaking up from behind like a common thief. Haven't even introduced myself, have I?" He stands up straight. "The name's Rider. I'm sorry to trespass on your land like this. The fact is, roads aren't safe for a man like me. Not with the guardsmen about, and me with no permit."

Tom blinks. "You don't have a permit?"

Rider smirks. "Never needed one. I've been all over this country, from one end to the other, without once setting foot on the King's roads."

I can tell that Tom is impressed. "How?"

"The sheep trails!" Rider gestures towards the mountains stretching high above us. "The old shepherd paths. Farmers used them for centuries to move their flocks, until the King banned it. They'll take you wherever you want, and faster than any road too."

Tom frowns. "But aren't they dangerous?"

Rider nods. "Course they are. There might not be guardsmen on those trails, but there's a hundred different ways to die up there. Fast fogs and faster rivers and worse. *Wolves* too."

He tugs at the pelt covering him, and I whine. The only thing that scares me more than a wolf is a human who can kill one. Tom leans down and rests a hand on my back to calm me.

"But you and I both know, boy, that there are far greater things to fear in this country than wolves. Things far more dangerous and bloodthirsty." Rider leans forward over the fence, his voice low and menacing. His eyes gleam like water hidden at the bottom of old wells. "I'm talking about the King. He's taken everything that's dear to us. And we've all grown so used to it that we let him keep on taking. But it doesn't have to be that way, does it?"

I feel Tom freeze beside me. Then Rider glances over his shoulder, and pulls down the collar of his shirt. There's a flash of red beneath it. He has a piece of cloth tied round his neck, hidden where it can't be seen.

Tom gasps. "You're with the Reds!"

Rider nods as he re-covers the neckerchief. "That's right. There are more of us too. More than you can imagine. Right now, there are thousands all over the country, waiting for the signal to rise together. A big change is coming. And when it's here, we'll need every pair of loyal hands we can find." Rider nods to Tom's drawing, dropped on the ground. "There's plenty of people who want the same as you. People who want to see the King thrown out of the High Castle. People who want our country back."

I whine and give a sharp bark. It's not safe for us to be speaking to Rider like this. We have to get rid of him!

But Tom doesn't seem frightened any more. He's looking at Rider the same way he looks at a storm cloud when it first appears over the mountains, his eyes wide with excitement.

Rider looks Tom up and down. "How old are you, boy?"

Tom hesitates before he answers. "Sixteen."

Sixteen?! And I'm a poodle! I bark at Tom reproachfully, but he doesn't even notice. Rider seems happy with the answer too.

"Sixteen! The Reds could do with a few smart sixteen-year-old lads like you. Not just as soldiers, either." He nods to the drawing. "People need to see what's possible. A picture like *that* could change people's minds faster than words ever could. And I do believe that you have a gift for that, Mister..."

He holds out his hand again. And this time, Tom takes it.

"Tom. My name's Tom."

I whine from the pit in my stomach, sticking close to Tom's heels and nudging him to make him stop. This is bad. Tom is shaking hands with a Red. If the guardsmen saw him now, they'd shoot him on sight. What is Tom doing? Why isn't he running?

Rider hunkers low over the fence, drawing Tom even closer. "There's a round ring of birch trees, twenty minutes north of here. Know the one?"

Tom nods. "By the river."

"That's right. There's a meeting happening there in an hour, for all new recruits. You coming?" He grins at Tom just like a wolf, full of hunger and cunning.

Tom pauses for a second before he answers. "I … I don't know…"

Rider's expression changes instantly, and his voice becomes a growl. "I thought I could trust you, Tom." He leans back from the fence, breaking their tight circle. "If we can't trust each other…"

Tom panics. "No! I'll come."

Rider grins again. "Glad to hear it. I'll lead the way." He nods at me. "And maybe leave your dog behind. He's a yappy one."

I growl. I do *not* like Rider.

Tom takes one final look at me, and starts to climb over the fence. I bark angrily. Tom can't be serious. He can't leave! We have to stay and look after the sheep!

"No, Rebel," says Tom, shooing me away. "You have to stay. I'll be back soon, OK?"

Stay? Of course I can't stay! Who'll protect him if something bad happens? I can't let him do this. I can't let him leave! I bark and whine, jumping up and scrabbling at his leg.

"No!" Tom snaps, pointing behind me. "*Stay*, Rebel."

I can't believe it. Tom wants to go without me. He wants to leave me behind.

But I'm a good dog, so I do what I'm told. I give him my best cold, hard stare, then sit down beside the fence. Tom stands halfway over it, looking guilty. "That's it. Good boy, Rebel."

My tail wags. He's right – I am a good boy.

Then Tom and Rider stride into the trees, and within seconds I can't see them any more. And that's it. I'm sat in Top Field *on my own*.

I can't think of the last time I was alone like this. Even when Tom goes to market, I'll stay in the farmhouse with Mum and whine at the window until he gets back. There's nothing to do. It's not like I can talk to the sheep. I have no idea how long it'll be until Tom returns. I might be waiting for *hours*.

But I'm a good dog. I come when Tom calls, and I stay when he tells me. Good dogs do what they're told.

So I wait.

5
UPRISING

And I wait.

And wait.

And wait.

The shadows are starting to stretch across the mountains. It's nearly sundown. If the guards find Tom outside now, he'll be arrested. The worry of it gnaws at me, like I've swallowed bad food.

I can hear Mum calling for Tom from the farmhouse. She's been calling for ages. We're late for dinner. Where is he? Why is he taking so long? *Oh, Tom, come back!*

I smell him before I see him – the charcoal under his fingernails and the conkers in his pockets catching on the wind that blows through the trees. I'm barking and running in circles before he even starts climbing over the fence. "Tom! Tom!"

"Shh, Rebel," he whispers.

But I can't help it. I'm just so happy to see him again. My tail wags so hard it bashes me in the face. "Never leave me again!" I cry.

I can tell that Tom's happy to see me too. He hugs me close, letting out a shuddering sigh of relief. I can taste the nervousness on him straight away. It hangs on him like heavy clothes. And I know *why* he's nervous too. The sheep should have been moved to Bottom Field hours ago. We're going to be in so, *so* much trouble.

Tom rounds up the sheep as fast as he can and drives them back to Bottom Field, then slams the gate behind him, and we race to the farmhouse and run through the door. I can sense the bad air the moment we step in the house. It's tight and dark, like the air inside a clenched fist.

Mum and Dad jump up from the table.

"Oh! Thank goodness!" cries Mum, hugging Tom tightly. "We were so worried!"

"Where have you been?" asks Dad quietly.

"Sorry!" replies Tom, a false light in his voice. "A sheep escaped. I had to go into the forest to find her."

I grumble uneasily. It's the second time that Tom's lied today. He's never fibbed so much before.

"It's past sundown!" Mum chides. "You know it's not safe to be outside so late."

"It won't happen again," he promises. "Now, what's for dinner – stew again, is it?"

"What is that?" says Dad. His voice is suddenly low and dangerous, like a knife being pulled from a belt.

I whine nervously, confused. I don't know what Dad's talking about at first, and neither does Tom. Then we all spot it.

A piece of red cloth is poking out of Tom's pocket, bright as a bloodstain.

The colour drains from Tom's face. Dad whips out the cloth and holds it up in his fist. "Tell me this isn't what I think it is," he growls.

Tom grabs it back. "It – it's nothing! I found it lying in the fields…"

"Liar!" hisses Dad, grabbing Tom by his shirt.

"Where have you been?"

I scurry under the table and lie down low to whine, but there's nowhere to hide. Bad feelings are pouring out of them and flooding the kitchen. I hate this – I hate this so much.

"Tom," Mum cries, "you *know* what that colour means! If the guardsmen found that on you, they'd kill you!"

Tom glares at her, his face growing hot and red. "So? They're going to kill us all eventually, no matter *what* we do! They'll tax us until we starve to death or shoot us in the streets for nothing. Better to die fighting than to lie down and take it!"

"Ha!" snorts Dad, but it's not a real laugh. "Don't care if you get shot, eh? What are you going to do next – march on the High Castle?"

"Yes!" Tom yells furiously. "That's *exactly* what I'm going to do!"

It silences the room.

"Tell me you're not being serious," says Dad at last, his voice as tense and deadly as a snare.

Tom takes a deep breath. His hands are trembling,

but he stands his ground. He seems taller all of a sudden.

"I swore an allegiance to the Reds tonight. We're going to rise up together, all over the country, and march through every village and town. We're going to gather all the people we can, and take back the roads. And when there are enough of us, we're going to march all the way to the High Castle and make the King listen to our demands!" He looks at Mum and Dad, his eyes shining. "There'll be twenty of us to every guardsman! The King will have to listen to what we say then. He'll see that we can't be pushed around any more. There won't be any more permits or double taxes…"

Mum is shaking her head. She's crying now. "Oh, Tom…"

Tom grabs her hand. "But I won't be fighting, Mum! The Reds don't just want soldiers – Rider says that I can draw posters to display in each village, to explain what we're going to do and—"

"Rider?" Dad snaps. "Who's Rider?"

Tom gulps, like he's trying to swallow back the words. "He – he's a brave man. And he likes my drawings, too. He thinks they can make a difference."

Dad almost shouts. "Drawings? You're going to go and get yourself killed over your stupid *drawings*?"

Tom shouts back, and I can hear that he's crying now, angry loud sobs that tear his voice apart. "I'd rather die than live here!"

Dad finally blows, and the argument starts proper. Dad screams at Tom, and Tom screams at Dad, and Mum screams at them both to stop. I can't stand it. I shoot up the stairs as fast as I can and burrow myself under the blankets to try to block out the noise, but it's impossible. I can hear Dad slamming his fists on the table, and Mum scraping and banging the chairs as she tries to get to Tom, and their voices shuddering up through the floorboards, all full of harsh angry words.

And then come the worst words of all.

"I hate you! I hate you!"

Tom's shout is so loud that I can hear him perfectly, even up here. His feet pound the stairs and he flies through the door, slamming it shut behind him and throwing himself face down on the bed.

Finally the house is quiet again. There's no sound except Tom's soft muffled sobs in the pillow.

There's only one thing I can do. I crawl from under the blankets and lie down beside him and close my eyes and let him feel my warmth, so he knows that I'm here. That he's not alone. That I love him.

It works. It always does. Tom reaches out and hugs me deep into him.

"Oh, Rebel," he cries, burying his face into my fur.

That's how we've always been, me and him. We've always been just what the other needs, ever since Tom first found me, alone in a ditch in the snow. He says I was so small he could hold me in the palm of his hand. He took one look at me and knew we'd be together for ever. I would be his dog, and he would be my boy.

So he tucked me into his coat and took me home. Mum and Dad tried to talk him out of it – they said that I was too sick, that trying to keep me alive was just cruel. But Tom wouldn't listen. He made me a little box of blankets and kept me by the fire so I was always warm, and he fed me milk and bread by hand and stayed with me night and day until I was finally better.

That's my very first memory. Snuggled up with Tom beside the fire while he feeds me, and knowing that it's all going to be OK, because Tom is there.

And now I do the same for him. I turn around and lick away his tears and let him know that it's all going to be fine. If I could talk, I would say, *Please don't cry. Tomorrow Mum and Dad will still love you. Tomorrow the sun will still shine. Tomorrow we'll sit in Top Field and you can draw whatever you want and we'll eat bacon for breakfast and lamb stew for dinner and all of this will be forgotten.*

I know Tom will be sad for a while. But Mum and Dad are right – staying at the farm is the right thing to do. Tomorrow he'll understand that. He'll forget about Rider, and the Reds, and the uprising, and everything will go back to the way it was.

Why would he want to change it, when it's already so perfect?

6
STAY

*N*o one knows how to begin the next day.

The house feels awful. It's like a rain cloud's swept in from the mountains and broken through the windows, weighing down the rooms with darkness and damp. I feel like I should stay in bed with Tom, but I can smell bacon downstairs, so I slink into the kitchen in case there's rind going spare. Tom means everything to me, but bacon is bacon.

Mum and Dad are sat at the table, waiting for Tom to come downstairs, but he takes much longer than normal. When he finally does, he's staring at the floor, letting his fringe hang low over his eyes.

"I'm sorry," he mumbles.

No one is expecting it. Even *I* wasn't expecting it.

"I'm not going to join the Reds," he continues. "I got overexcited. Let's … let's just pretend none of it happened, OK?" He looks up guiltily. "Please."

The tension breaks, like a crack in the clouds. Mum stands up and hugs him. She looks like she's about to cry again, which I don't understand, because this is good news – Tom is staying here, where he belongs!

Dad's face floods with relief. He takes Tom's hand and squeezes it tightly. "I didn't mean to lose my temper like that. I just… I *know* people who died fighting the King, Tom. People who got taken away. I couldn't lose you like that. I couldn't bear it." He grips Tom's hand even tighter. "We'll bury that neckerchief in Bottom Field. We'll make sure the guardsmen never find out that you went to that meeting."

Tom shakes his head. "It's already gone. I threw it in the fire last night."

I glance at him. I didn't see Tom throw *anything* in the fire. He must have done it while I was sleeping. But I would have noticed, wouldn't I?

It doesn't matter – everything is fixed, back to normal. I can feel the love flowing between Tom and

Mum and Dad again, like sunlight shining through trees. The house is still sore, still bruised, but I know it will heal.

The rest of the morning is perfect. The sky's as bright as a blue ribbon and the fields are alive with bugs and flutter-bys. The whole world is an open flower, full and fragrant; you could spend a whole day sitting in the same spot, and you'd never smell the same scent twice. Dad chats and jokes to Tom all morning, rubbing his back as they work. It's like he's gained a whole new son.

But I can tell that Tom's mind is elsewhere. He laughs along with Dad, but whenever Dad looks away, Tom's smile disappears and he glances up at the sky. I don't understand what he's looking at – there's nothing up there but blue sky and bright sun. He must still be feeling sad about the argument.

Soon lunch is finished, and Tom and I are alone in Top Field, watching the sheep as they scour the scrub. This is it; our best bit of the day. I'm so excited that I run around, barking and barking, and find a stick for Tom to throw.

But Tom doesn't throw it. He's not even looking at

me. He's watching Dad as he makes his way back to the farmhouse. Then he glances up at the sky again, as if checking for something. What's going on?

Tom walks over to the fence and starts to climb. He takes the knapsack off his back. Then he opens it, and pulls something out from inside.

My heart drops. It's the red neckerchief. The one from last night. Tom didn't get rid of it after all. He lied to Mum and Dad. *Again!*

And then *he puts the neckerchief on!*

"Stay, Rebel," he whispers. "That's a good boy."

Suddenly I understand why Tom's been looking at the sun all day. He's been trying to check the time. He's going to another meeting in the forest! He's going to see Rider again!

This is too much. I can't let Tom ruin everything, right after it's been fixed. I run at him and bark as loud as I can. "No! Don't go!"

"Rebel, *no*," says Tom, not understanding me. "You can't come. You need to stay."

I won't let him go! I bark and bark, jumping up and biting at his trousers to drag him back.

"No!" Tom suddenly shouts, his eyes bright with anger. "Bad dog!"

I fall back in dismay. *Bad dog?* How can he say that? I'm trying to help him. I'm trying to keep him safe. All I've ever done is love him. How can he tell me I'm bad?

Tom points behind me. "Go over there! Now!"

I can't believe this. I slink away with my head hung low and my heart aching. This is awful. For the first time ever, I don't know how to help Tom. Everything is changing and I don't know how to stop it.

I almost can't bring myself to look at him. When I do, Tom is straddling the fence, half on one side and half on the other. He's staring at me, and he looks so sad. And I can't help it – my tail starts wagging again. I should be angry at him for lying, and for breaking the rules, and for shouting at me, but it's no use. I love him too much.

Tom jumps off the fence and starts walking back to me. My tail wags even harder. He's changed his mind! Maybe he's going to ruffle my head and say, *Hey, Rebel, I'm sorry for shouting. I actually hate Rider and I'm not going into the forest after all; let's stay here and chase sticks*

and gaze at the mountains until it's time for stew. Let's do
that every single day forever and ever until the day we die.

But Tom doesn't do that. Instead he removes the red
cloth from his neck, kneels down and ties it around me
like a collar.

"Good boy, Rebel," he says softly. "You're such
a good boy."

My tail thumps the ground. I *am* a good boy! But
Tom doesn't look happy – in fact, he almost looks like
he's crying. He wipes his eyes and his nose, like he used
to when he was a little boy, and strokes my head a final
time, oh so gently.

"Stay," he says again.

And then he stands up and walks away without
looking back. He climbs swiftly over the fence and runs
into the forest, getting smaller and smaller until he's so
tiny that I can't see him any more.

I'm shocked. I thought Tom was going to stay with
me because he was sad. He *always* comes to me when
he's sad. But he ran off – and he didn't even take his
neckerchief with him. Maybe he's gone to tell Rider that
he's changed his mind, and he won't be coming to any

more meetings after all. That makes sense. Tom feels bad for shouting at me, and so he's going to tell Rider to leave him alone from now on.

He took his knapsack with him, though. I wonder why.

For a moment, I think about following him … but then I stop myself. Tom told me to wait here until he comes back, so that's exactly what I'll do. I'm a good dog, and I do what Tom tells me. Because I love him.

I wait.

7
DARKNESS

And I wait.

And wait.

And wait.

And wait.

It's full night. It's dark and cold. There aren't even shadows on the hill any more. Mum and Dad have been calling Tom's name for hours. A bitter wind is blowing from the mountains, so loud that I can barely hear the sheep bleating beside me.

"Cold," they cry. "Cold, hungry, scared, cold."

They were supposed to be in Bottom Field hours ago. They know something's wrong. They're huddled together and shaking. I'm shaking too, but I don't think it's from the cold.

Tom hasn't come back. That means something must be wrong. A million things could have happened to him. And now that I've started imagining them, I can't stop.

What if he's lost? That could happen easily in the dark.

What if he's fallen and can't get up? He'll be cold and hurt and frightened.

What if he's decided to find me a treat on the way home? I like that one, but I don't think it's true.

What if a guardsman's caught him and he's been arrested? I don't want to think about that. I just want him back. I want it with all my everything. Where *is* he?

The wind drops for a moment, and I hear a sound from the farmhouse. This time, it's not Mum calling for him.

It's a scream.

Something bad has happened at the farm: Mum or Dad could be in trouble. I can't stay here, not any more. Tom would want me to go and help.

I race down the hill as fast as I can, leaping over the gate and scrambling through the half-open farmhouse door, and I see that things are really, really bad. Mum is face down on the table, sobbing; Dad is wearing his big coat. He must have been outside, looking for Tom.

"Love, what's happened?" Dad's shouting, almost begging. "What is it?"

Mum sits up, her face streaming with tears. She gulps in big deep breaths, trying to calm herself enough to reply. "I – I found it under his pillow…"

She's clutching something in her trembling hand. It's a piece of paper from Tom's sketchpad. There's charcoal writing on it. Dad's face crumples up, because he can't read the words like Mum and Tom can.

"What does it say?" He holds her shoulders gently. "Love, please, I need to know."

Mum takes a few more deep breaths and holds up the paper. When she talks it comes out fast, like when the river high above us in the mountains breaks in the storm and all the water comes tumbling down Top Field.

"Mum, Dad, I'm sorry that I had to lie to you but I promise that one day you will be glad I done it. When I'm back, it will all have been worth it and the country will be ours again. I love—" Her voice breaks. *"I love—"*

She starts crying again and rests her head on the

table, letting the letter drop to the floor. Dad doesn't pick it up. He just stays where he is, white as sheep's bone, too shocked to speak.

Tom can't have written that. He would never run away. He would never leave home. I run over to the letter to smell it, to make sure it's really him that wrote it, and not some imposter – Rider perhaps...

But then I see that it's not just words in the letter. Tom's done one of his drawings at the bottom, too. No one can draw like he does.

It's him, standing on the tallest tower of the King's High Castle. He's holding a red flag, which flies big and proud in the sky. The gorge below him is filled with people, all waving banners and swords and spears and cheering for him.

But this drawing is different from the last one he made.

Because I'm not in it.

THE
WORST
DAY

8

CHOICE

I don't know how I make it through the next day.

I wake up in bed alone. I slept here so I could be near Tom's smell, but it's not the same without him. It's cold and sad and empty.

Mum is downstairs by herself. There's no bacon at breakfast, and no Dad. He left late last night to look for Tom and still hasn't come home. Mum's face is red and puffy from crying. Everything is wrong. Everything is different. It's awful, awful, awful.

I pace the house until Dad comes home. He looks exhausted. He's walked all the way to Connick and back, but he says there's no sign of Tom anywhere.

He barely talks after that. Neither does Mum. They both smell like sadness, a scent that clings to them and doesn't let go. I whine and paw at Dad's feet – the sheep have been out in Top Field all night, and no one's brought them back down. But Dad doesn't even notice me. He's staring at the table, looking at things that aren't there.

I can't bear it. I leave the house and walk around the farm in a blurred haze. The weather is perfect. It's another pure and beautiful day: the farm is at its very best, and Tom isn't even here to enjoy it. He's gone, and I don't know where he is. This is already the longest that he and I have ever been apart.

Then, all of sudden, I catch his scent on the wind. For a moment, my heart leaps – Tom's come back! Then I realize it's just the scent he left on the ground when he walked through Bottom Field yesterday. I dig my nose deep into the earth and drink it in. There he is, pressed between a million other smells: his hair, his skin, the charcoal under his nails and the conkers in his pockets, all of him Tom. Tomorrow, or the day after maybe, the scent will start to fade. It'll be worn down by wind and rain and scrubbed to nothing.

I follow the scent up to Top Field. The sheep are still

here, bleating miserably. I stand by the fence where I last saw Tom and gaze into the forest. It looks so deep and dark in there. I can't believe I let him go alone.

I feel a flash of anger at myself. *Why* did I let him go? I should have found a way to make him stay. I should have showed him how perfect everything is on the farm, to make him see how he never needs to leave it, not ever. I should have done *something*.

I know exactly what to do now. I sit down on the grass, facing the trees, and I wait.

"What on *earth* are you doing?"

Priscilla is sprawled amongst some wild flowers near by, gazing at me in disgust.

"I'm sitting down," I say. Priscilla really is stupid sometimes.

"I know *that*," she mutters, licking her paw. "I'm talking about that silly red rag around your neck."

It takes me a moment to realize what she's talking about. I'm still wearing the neckerchief from yesterday. "Tom gave it to me. Mum and Dad are too sad to take it off."

"Why don't *you* take it off?"

"Because Tom gave it to me," I repeat. "And I'm going to wait here wearing it until he gets back. So he'll know I stayed, like he told me to. Because I'm a good dog and I love him."

Priscilla gawps at me. Then she rolls in the wild flowers and howls with laughter. It's the first time I've ever seen her properly laugh.

"What's so funny?" I ask.

Priscilla stretches, turning her body into one big curve. "You might find you'll be waiting rather a long time," she says curtly.

I fume. "I don't care! I'll wait as long as I have to. A whole day. *Two* days, even!"

Priscilla looks at me in surprise. "Wow. You really don't understand what's going on, do you?" She sits down and faces me. "Tom has joined the Reds. The Reds are going to rise up against the King. It could become a war. You know what *war* means, don't you?"

"When people fight each other."

"Not just fighting, Rebel," says Priscilla more gently. "*Dying.* People die in wars."

It feels like the whole world has frozen around me.

Like everything in the field is bald blank snow, except for me and Priscilla.

"N-no," I stammer. "Tom wouldn't do that. He wouldn't *die*."

"He might not have a choice, Rebel."

The awful truth begins to dawn on me. Tom might not be coming back soon. He might not come back *ever*. I'll never see him again. We'll never chase each other and play with sticks and lie in the sun. I'll never hear his voice say *Little Belly*. His bed will always be cold, and his chair will always be empty. His smell will fade like morning frost.

Priscilla sighs with pity. "Listen, farm dog. I know we've never got on, but I'm going to give you some advice." She prowls towards me. "Forget about Tom. Forget about being his dog. Don't put your love in humans. It never works out. Just be *you*. You're young enough to change." She nods to the farm. "You have a great deal here. You have food, somewhere warm to sleep. The farmer will look after you when you're old, and then you'll die happy and well fed. That's worth more than you might think."

I shake my head. "It won't mean anything. Not without Tom."

Priscilla rolls her eyes. "Good grief! All this for some *master*..."

"He's *not* my master!" I shout furiously. "He's my friend. He *needs* me."

"Humans don't need dogs, Rebel."

"Tom does!" I shout again. "He needs me to be there when he's sad or frightened. He needs me to make him sit down and look at the sunset sometimes. He needs me to remember how beautiful everything is."

She sighs. "Humans need more than that."

"No, they don't," I say. "They think they do, but they don't."

Priscilla gives a sorry shake of her head, and turns away from me with a flick of her tail. "Very well. Then let me leave you with this, farm dog: if Tom *really* is your friend, and not your master, then why are you still obeying him?"

With that, she slinks gracefully down the hillside and out of sight.

I stay where I am, staring at the forest. I want to

tell Priscilla that she's wrong. Tom has never been my master. He is my *everything*. He's my nights and my mornings and all my hours in between.

But I know, deep down in my heart, that she's right. I *am* still obeying him, like he's my master. Waiting here might make me a good dog, but it isn't going to bring him back.

If he really is my friend, then I have to protect him. I have to fight for him. I have to show him how much I love him. I have to save him, like he saved me.

So I'm not going to do what he told me to do any more. I'm not going to sit and stay like a good boy.

I'm going to get him back.

9

CROSSING

I stand up, my heart pounding as I sniff the ground. Tom's scent is still there, trailing beneath the fence and twisting through the forest. If I follow it now, while it's still fresh, it'll lead me straight to Tom. I can find him and bring him back home.

All I have to do is leave the farm.

I feel fear like a pair of paws pressed against my chest, pushing me back. I've never even been through the front gate before. Everything I've ever needed has always been right here, right where I belong. Top Field, Bottom Field, the farmyard, the house, Tom's bed…

I glance over my shoulder and gaze at it all. The farm has never looked more beautiful. But until Tom comes back, it will never be perfect again.

Because if he saved me when I was a puppy, then who else but me can save him now?

I take a deep breath, scrabble up my courage, and crawl under the fence. And with that, I've left home. I'm the furthest away I've ever been. It feels weird, like when you swim in muddy water and have no idea how much deeper it goes beneath you.

I press my nose to the ground. There's the smell of Tom, winding through the forest like a golden thread. I follow it, racing through the trees and sticking close to his scent. It's not always easy to find. After all, there are thousands of other smells here: fir, pine, wet stone, leaf mould, birds and more. I can sense where rabbits have crossed the path, where stoats have marked the trees, where something once lay down and died. But I keep following the trace until I find exactly what I'm searching for.

Another scent: burnt wood, ash, churned earth. It's the smell of a campfire lit here last night and covered over. I can smell maybe twenty other people too – their clothes, their sweat, their oily boots, their pipe tobacco.

My tail wags. *This* must be the meeting place where Rider took Tom. Wherever the Reds have gone, they'll have started from here. All I have to do is follow their trail. The scent is easy to track now: twenty people make a lot of stink, and Tom's golden thread has joined it. I follow it through the trees, my heart racing as I run faster and faster and the scent gets stronger and stronger. I'm catching up!

After a while, the forest ends, and the trees are cut off by an old stone road. There's no one on it now – it's silent and empty. Tom's scent leads right down it. That makes sense – he said that the Reds were going to march from village to village, gathering supporters as they went to take back the roads.

But I can smell something else too. Rat and Slug, the stench of their musket powder staining the ground where they walked past a couple of days ago. My hackles rise and a growl begins low in my throat. The Reds are taking a huge risk by leaving the forest and walking along this road. If they run into any guardsmen now, they'll be shot on sight. The uprising will be over before it's even started. Tom could die.

I have to catch up with them before that happens. I race down the road, my heart thundering. I'm coming, Tom!

I run for what feels like hours, my nose pressed tight to the ground, but I don't pass a single person. I can smell dozens of different wagons and horses, though – after a while, the smells start to become busier, tangled up with each other like overgrown weeds. Soon there's so many that it's almost impossible to find Tom's scent amongst them.

I can hear noises too – *lots* of noises. People. My heart lifts. Have I caught up with the Reds? Is Tom just ahead of me? I run even faster, turning a final bend … and come to a grinding halt.

I can't believe what I'm seeing. I'm so shocked that my tail droops and I have to sit down for a moment. There are buildings lining the road ahead. But I've never seen so many before. There must be … I mean, there could be *ten* of them!

I shake my head in disbelief. This must be Connick, the village where Tom and Dad go to market. I can see wagons piled high with chickens, baskets of vegetables, barrels of potatoes packed in dirt. There are people too – more people than I've ever seen in my life. They're hanging washing from the windows, carrying baskets up and down the road, scrubbing their doorsteps, beating dust out of their blankets. I've never seen so many *things* happening all at the same time.

It's amazing. I had no idea there was so much *life* out here, away from the farm.

But something feels *wrong*. There's a strange atmosphere hanging over the village like damp fog. No one is talking. No one's even looking at one another. It's like the whole village is trying to hide something, trying to keep a secret while they know they're being watched.

And where's Tom? There's no sign of him. I keep to the edge of the road and follow the fraying thread of his scent, following it past more wagons and buildings...

Then I stop. I'm standing at a crossing in the centre of the village. Tom's smell has been getting harder and harder to follow since I arrived here – there are too many other smells jumbled on top of it – but now, all of a sudden, in the middle of the road, it disappears.

I run around frantically, trying to find it again, but it's no use. The scent trail stops dead, right in the middle of the crossroads. It's vanished into thin air.

Tom's gone.

10

SEAMUS

"Well, well!" says a voice behind me. "Looks like someone's having an even worse day than I am. Which is a miracle, considering I'm about to be turned into sausages."

I spin around, but there's nothing except an old wagon.

"Up here."

I look up into the big beaming face of a pig. He's poking his snout through the bars of a cage not much bigger than he is.

"That's right!" He sighs heavily. "It's the end of the line for poor old Seamus. Thanks to these new double taxes, the farmer can't afford to keep me any more, so I'm off to market to be sold. I'll be carved up for sausages before the day is out!" He shakes his head sorrowfully. "*Sausages.* And to think my grandfather was a prize-winning Westchester boar. Have you ever heard of anything so tragic?"

I don't know how to answer, because I don't know what a Westchester boar is. In fact, I've only understood about three words of what Seamus has said.

"Can you help me?" I ask. "My name's Rebel. I'm looking for someone."

Seamus brightens up. "Well! You've come to the right pig! I'm something of a virtuoso when it comes to faces. Nothing gets past old Seamus! Why don't you hop up onto the wagon and have a chat?"

My tail wags. If Seamus is good at remembering faces, he might have seen where Tom went. Hopping up onto the wagon is easier said than done, though. It's a big wagon, and I'm a small dog. I manage it on my third try.

"Ah! That's better," exclaims Seamus. "Now we're on a level!"

I've never met a pig like Seamus before. Come to think of it, I've never met a *pig* before – not formally, anyway. He has a bright bristly tuft of orange hair, and a tusk that juts out of his mouth like a pipe. His big floppy ears keep falling over his eyes. He smells like old pickles and hot soup.

"So, this boy that I'm looking for…" I begin.

"Yes, of course!" says Seamus quickly. "Very happy to help, Rebel old chap. But, er … speaking as one animal in need to another, perhaps we can help each other out. You scratch my back, I'll scratch yours, eh?"

I don't know how I'm going to scratch Seamus's back if he's in a cage, but if it means I find Tom, I'll do anything. I nod.

"Splendid!" says Seamus. "You see, I'm somewhat keen to avoid being butchered. There's normally not a pigpen in the country that can hold old Seamus! Believe you me, I've made more breaks for freedom than you've hot dinners."

I wag my tail again. I love hot dinners.

Seamus taps the lock on the cage with his trotter. "Sadly, this contraption is proving a little trickier than normal. So perhaps we can strike a deal. You help me escape, and I'll help you find your friend!"

"Sure," I say.

"Fabulous! Let's get to work. Firstly, tell me about this boy of yours. Any defining features? Tattoos, eyepatch, wooden leg, that kind of thing?"

I open my mouth … but nothing comes out. How can I describe Tom? It's like trying to describe the sun. Nothing comes even close to explaining how it feels to be with him.

"He's twelve, but tall for his age. He has scruffy brown hair. Um…" Something suddenly comes to me. "And he won't have been alone! He'd have been with lots of people all wearing red neckerchiefs. And a man in a wolfskin…"

Seamus perks up instantly. "I remember that chap well! You don't forget a sight like that, let me tell you." He points a trotter down the road. "They passed through here late last night, heading towards Drulter. Half the village went with them! The wolfskin man made everyone climb into the back of wagons, you see, and hide between crates of fruit and veg bound for Drulter market. Then he covered them all up with old blankets. Only the wagon drivers get their permits checked, so it means they'll be able to sneak past right under the guardsmen's noses. Job done!"

My tail wags harder than ever. What a clever idea! That explains why I can't smell Tom any more. He's climbed into a wagon!

Then my tail droops as I realize what that means. If the wagons left late last night, then Tom's already hours ahead of me. How am I supposed to catch up with him?

Seamus seems to read my mind. "Never fret, Rebel my lad. This wagon's bound for Drulter too – stay on board, and you'll catch up with your boy sooner or later!"

I shake my head. "It won't be quick enough. By the time I arrive, Tom could have moved on again."

Seamus grunts wisely. "Hmm. You've got your work cut out for you there, old chap. There's only one road through these mountains, and that's the one we're standing on."

I frown. Something about what Seamus has just said doesn't seem right.

"Wait – that isn't true. There *is* another way…"

I'm not always good at remembering things. I *can* do it, but only if I try really hard. I have to try hard now.

I close my eyes, focusing all my thoughts on what Rider said to Tom…

The sheep trails. They'll take you wherever you want, and faster than any road too.

My eyes snap open. "Seamus – is there a sheep trail that leads out of Connick?"

"One of the old mountain paths? Just over there, old boy."

He points his snout towards a narrow gap between two houses on the other side of the road. You could walk right past without spotting it: it's just a thin rubbly path, blocked up with old planks of wood painted with red warnings. The trail twists up the steep slope, all the way to the top of the mountain.

I bark with excitement. I can't help it. The answer's right in front of me. The sheep trails! *That's* how I can catch up with Tom. I can follow the path all the way to Drulter and get there before it's too late!

"Thank you, Seamus!"

The pig beams. "Delighted to help! Now, er … back to our agreement." He taps a trotter on the cage. "Couldn't help an old pig break free, could you?"

I've forgotten all about that. I look at the cage nervously. I've never opened one before. How am I supposed to do it?

"It's simple!" says Seamus, reading my mind again. "See that wooden bar there? That's held in place with this old rope. Get your gnashers around that, pull it loose, slide the bar free, and Bob's your uncle."

I'm confused. I don't have an uncle. Who's Bob? But I promised I'd help Seamus, so I grab the rope and start gnawing at it, tugging with my jaws until it starts to fray.

"That's it!" encourages Seamus, dancing on his trotters. "That's the stuff, Rebel my lad! Keep going for old Seamus…"

I yank again, and the rope snaps. Now for the wooden bar. I carefully bite down on it, jemmy it loose with my head, then pull it to one side… *Click!* The bar slides free and the cage door swings open.

"You did it!" cries Seamus. "There's a good lad!"

I wag my tail happily. I did do it! I *am* a good lad!

"*Oi!*"

A man is charging up the road towards us, waving

a stick. I wonder if it's Bob. I don't want him to be my uncle – he looks furious.

"Ah," mutters Seamus. "That's the farmer. Time to make ourselves scarce."

I don't need telling twice. I leap off the wagon, racing to the entrance to the sheep trail before anyone can stop me. Seamus flies down the road in the other direction, away from the farmer.

"Thank you, Seamus!" I cry.

"And good luck to you, Rebel!" Seamus calls back. "All the luck in the world!"

I gulp. I'm going to need it. Leaving the farm is one thing, but heading into the mountains? Rider's words echo in my head.

There's a hundred different ways to die up there. Fast fogs and faster rivers and worse. Wolves too.

I feel my ears press flat to my head. *Wolves!* My actual worst nightmare. Am I really going to do this?

But I have to. If the sheep trails are the only way I can reach Tom, then that's the way I'm going. I'd fight a hundred wolves and climb a thousand mountains to bring him home.

I hold Tom in my heart, take a deep breath, and race up the path to the point where the peak becomes the sky.

11
TRAIL

*R*unning up the trail is different from running on the road. The road is straight and flat and cobbled; the trail is steep and twisty and made of sharp little stones that hurt my paws. Before long, I'm exhausted.

But whenever I feel myself slowing down, I think of Tom chasing me or tickling my belly or sharing his breakfast with me, and it spurs me on to go faster.

Soon the trail starts to level out. I can finally see the slope crest where it reaches the top of the mountain. I push myself for the last stretch, racing to the summit...

And stop.

I have no words for the hugeness of what lies in front of me.

I've always thought you can see the whole world from Top Field. Turns out I'm wrong. *Dead* wrong.

The mountain that I'm standing on is just one part of a long chain of mountains. They link all the way to the horizon, one after the other, until they fade beyond where I can see. Tucked between each one is a patchwork of fields and valleys and forests and rivers, darkened by great streaks of shadow where clouds cross the sun. Even the sky is like a landscape up here; you can spin in a circle and the sky is still there, whichever way you look. How did I not realize that all of this was up here?

And the *smell*. My heart pounds like a jackhammer as I drink it all in. It's deeper and sweeter than anything I've ever smelled in my life. Fresh water and horseflies and birds and beetles…

And something else. Something that smells *amazing*. My mouth waters just sniffing it. It's a herb that looks like clover, but smells sweet as fresh apples. All of a sudden I realize how hungry I am – I haven't eaten all day. I pull up a mouthful of leaves and chew them; the moment I do, a bolt of sourness zaps across my tongue like lightning. My whole head fizzes. I've never tasted anything like it.

I gobble down as much as I can, and before long I feel full of energy again. I turn back to the trail as it twists along the mountain top like a strand of hair. Somewhere along that is the path to Drulter.

"I'm coming, Tom!" I bark.

I race along the trail with the wind in my fur. I already feel like I'm closer to him. I can't wait to see him again!

But then the path suddenly becomes *two* paths, splitting like a cut branch. One heads left; the other heads right. There's an old wooden sign stuck between them. I can't read what it says, because wild moss has grown over it and covered up all the words. Also because I'm a dog.

I'm stumped. I have no idea which path is the right one. I lower my head and sniff the ground for clues. I can smell sheep and rabbits and deer ... and something else too, something I don't recognize. It's like a dog, but different. Bigger. Dirtier. Wilder.

A wolf?

The hair stands on end all over my body. I have no idea what wolves smell like. I've always imagined they'd smell like fire, all brutal and dark and angry… What if there's one on the path ahead?

I can't stand around – I have to get off this mountain and find Tom, as fast as I can. There's a patch of that special clover growing beside me. I eat another load of it for energy, choose the path leading left and start to run. But after a while the way becomes narrower and trickier … then it stops being a path at all. I get the feeling this isn't right, but I don't want to go all the way back up to the fork. I'm already hours behind Tom; I need to keep going.

The sky suddenly booms above me, and I jump. The beautiful sunshine has disappeared, and now thunder is pacing the sky like an animal. The weather changes fast up here; it's going to start raining soon. What am I going to do?

That's when I feel a fist of pain twist inside my belly. It comes so fast that it almost stops me in my tracks. I slow down. My stomach hurts, *bad*. I'm starting to feel really weird, like I'm full of muggy water, but my mouth is dry as old bones. My vision blurs and I blink. My eyes are burning in my head like hot coals.

I don't think that clover was special after all.

Water. I need water. I spot a brook a short distance from the trail and almost tumble down the slope in my hurry to drink. I lap gingerly at the water, but it does nothing to ease the pain in my guts or the hammering in my head. It feels like I've swallowed a bag of nails. Can things get any worse?

The rain falls at once, in a great burst. Within seconds, I'm soaked through. I have to find shelter. But there's *nothing*. I'm high up on the mountainside, with hardly anything between me and the sky. The whole world is rain, from edge to edge. I'm sick, and lost, and exhausted.

I try to take a step forward, and collapse on the ground. I can't move. I think I might be dying.

So I do the only thing that makes sense. I close my eyes and dream about Tom.

We're in Top Field together. It's a perfect day, like always. We're chasing each other, and I'm so happy. I find a stick for Tom to throw for me.

But all of a sudden, Tom turns away and runs across Top Field. He can't take my stick because he's carrying a big red flag that flutters in the wind behind him.

"Tom! Come back!" I try to shout. But I can't, because of the stick in my mouth. I try to spit it out but the stick just keeps getting bigger and heavier.

Tom runs into the forest and I follow him, but I can't keep up. The stick is now so big that it keeps getting wedged between the trees. All I can do is watch as Tom gets smaller and smaller.

"Tom! Don't leave me!" I try to shout.

And now I'm getting smaller and smaller too. I'm a puppy again, lying in a wooden box, watching Tom leave the room. I shout and shout, but Tom won't listen because I'm a dog and he doesn't understand.

"Come back! Please!" I beg.

"Shh," says a soft, gruff voice.

I look blearily to one side. There's a wolf sitting on the ground beside me, big and old and grey and solemn. I should be terrified, but for some reason I'm not. Besides, I couldn't run if I wanted to. I can't move a single muscle.

"It's just a dream," says the wolf. "Try to save your strength."

I don't care what the wolf says. I can't let Tom get away!

"Tom! Tom!"

Why can't he hear me? Why won't he come back?

12

JAXON

I open my eyes. That was a mistake. I close them again.

Then I open them once more. *Slowly.*

I groan with misery. I have never felt this bad, not ever. Not even when I ate that thing floating in the puddle in Bottom Field. My blood is like hot vinegar. My skull feels like it's packed with gravel and thorns. I gaze around. It's already morning – I must have lost half a day lying here. What am I going to do?

"You're awake," growls a voice beside me.

I twist my head. Something is sitting next to me. Something big, and dark, and shaggy...

A wolf! It wasn't a dream – there really is a wolf, right beside me!

The burst of terror gives me enough energy to try to

run, but it doesn't work because I'm still too weak. The second I get to my feet, I fall over again.

Luckily, it's not a wolf. It's a dog – but he's *massive*. He has deep, dark fur and sharp ears with a chunk taken out of one. His voice is deep and growly, like rocks rubbing against each other. He looks like he's made from rock too – strong and hard and grey and cold.

"You're lucky I found you when I did," he says. "I only stopped to get water for the night and there you were." He picks something up from the ground and drops it in front of me. "Eat this."

It's a dead rabbit, its thick fur clotted with blood. The knot in my stomach clenches tighter.

"Do it," orders the dog. "You need your strength."

I really, *really* do not want to eat the rabbit. I don't even know how to. I lick tentatively at the blood around its neck, and to my surprise, I feel better instantly. I lap at the blood hungrily, energy growing like a big bright flower inside me.

"Let me guess," says the dog. "You ate something bad?"

I open my mouth, but it's so dry that my voice comes out as a croak. *"Special clover…"*

"Sorrel. It's poisonous for dogs. Don't eat it again. Can you stand up?"

My legs are still weak, but the rabbit has really helped. I get shakily to my feet.

"Good," says the dog. "Now, do yourself a favour. Head back the way you came and return home. Take it slow and beg for food as you go. You look like you'd be good at that. Keep the rabbit."

With that, he splashes over the brook and climbs up to the trail. A faint thought pushes through the fog in my head, making its way slowly to the top. "Wait... Do you know the way to Drulter?"

The dog stops and turns around. "That's what the humans call it, yes. Why?"

My heart lifts. I might not be too late after all! My tail wags feebly, but I make it stop, because I really don't have the strength for that right now.

"What's your name?" I ask.

The dog stares at me. "Why?"

"So I can ask you something."

"You can do that without knowing my name."

"Yes, but it's more polite."

The dog shifts on his paws irritably. "Jaxon. My name's Jaxon."

"Hello, Jaxon," I say. "I'm Rebel. I need you to take me to Drulter, please."

Jaxon stares at me for a while. Maybe it's the illness, but I swear I can almost hear him blink.

"Sorry," he says eventually. "For a moment, it sounded like you asked me to take you to Drulter."

"I did," I say. "As quick as you can, please. I'm in a bit of a hurry."

Jaxon stares at me for a while longer. Then he turns around and starts walking up the slope again.

"Hey – where are you going?" I call after him.

"Not to Drulter," says Jaxon. "And neither are you. You're going to eat the rest of that rabbit, and then you're going to go home."

I panic. I can't let him leave – he's my only hope of finding Tom! I stagger weakly after him. "Please! You have to help me! If I don't get to Drulter in time, I'm going to lose Tom for ever!"

"Who's Tom?"

"My boy."

Jaxon snorts with derision. "That's your problem, farm dog. I'm not beholden to humans. And I'm not your servant, either. Goodbye."

Jaxon keeps walking away from me. And suddenly I feel myself fill with rage. I don't care that he's three times my size. I don't care how weak and sick I am. I start to follow him, barking as loudly as I can.

"Fine! If you won't help me, I'll find Drulter on my own, you … you bad dog!"

Jaxon spins around, his lips curled in a snarl … and stops.

"You're standing in the brook," he tells me.

"I know!" Of course I do; I'm up to my chest and it's absolutely freezing.

"You should probably get out."

"I know!" I say, still not moving.

Jaxon suddenly looks sorry for me. "Look – I'll do you a favour. Tell me where you've come from, and I'll show you the quickest way back. If you stay here, you're going to die. The mountains aren't kind to stupid dogs."

The solution comes to me in a flash. "Yes! I'll die

and it'll be all your fault! I'll stay in this brook and eat sorrel until it's coming out of my ears!"

Jaxon grinds his teeth. "I'm not taking you to Drulter."

"Suit yourself." I sit down in the brook and give him my best hard stare.

Jaxon looks at me, up to my neck in water, teeth chattering. Then he looks at the ground, and then up at the sky, and gives one of those long, deep sighs that sound a bit like a scream.

"Fine," he snaps. "But after that, you're on your own."

I startle. For a moment, I don't believe my ears. "You're taking me to Drulter? Really?!"

"Yes," says Jaxon wearily. "I'm not beholden to humans, but I *am* beholden to dogs in trouble. And you, Rebel, are in more trouble than any dog I've ever met. It's a miracle you're still alive."

I can't believe it. My plan's worked. And all because I pretended I'm stupid!

"Thank you, Jaxon!"

"You might want to get out of that brook now."

"Oh, yes." I'm glad he said that. I'm freezing. I clamber out and shake myself dry.

"Bring the rabbit too."

"Good idea!" I paddle back and grab the rabbit and then race after Jaxon, trying to keep up as best as I can. My heart is pounding, and not because I nearly died last night. I'm not lost any more. I'm back on the trail. I can still save Tom!

"Thank you for helping me," I say. "I really appreciate it. Tom would be so grateful if he knew. So would Mum and Dad! Priscilla wouldn't, but that's just because she's a cat. The sheep would thank you, though! There are lots of them. Kitty and Agnes and Mabel—"

"Rebel?"

"Yes?"

"Stop talking or I'll change my mind."

13
COMPANIONS

We run along the trail together. I try to keep up with Jaxon, but it's impossible. He's much bigger than I am, and his legs are longer and stronger too. Besides, I still feel terrible after eating that sorrel. After a while, Jaxon stops and watches me catch up.

"Is that the fastest you can run?" he asks.

I want to answer but I'm too busy trying not to pass out.

"Fine," Jaxon sighs. "We'll walk. It means we won't get to Drulter until tomorrow, though."

I shake my head. "No! That could be too late! I've already lost a whole day as it is..."

"Either we're late," says Jaxon gruffly, "or you push yourself too hard and we don't get there at all. What'll it be?"

I groan. Jaxon's right – I can't afford to be ill again.

He sets off once more, but this time at a trot. I follow meekly behind him. I still have to scramble to keep up, but it's better than before.

"So," I say, trying to fill the silence. "You're a mountain dog."

Jaxon glances at me. "I thought you weren't going to talk."

"What *else* are we going to do to pass the time?"

Jaxon makes a small noise at the back of his throat.

"So," I try again, "what's your favourite part of the mountains?"

"The silence."

"Me too!" I agree. "And the space! I've never seen so much space before. You could probably go weeks without seeing another dog up here. You must get really lonely."

Jaxon shakes his head. "I never get lonely. I'm one of the Masterless."

I blink. "What's a Masterless?"

He holds himself slightly taller. "Dogs that live without masters. Dogs that have never seen the inside of a house, or eaten from a bowl, or been forced to do tricks."

I'm amazed. "You've *never* lived with a human?"

Jaxon snorts. "Following orders? Begging for food? Doesn't sound like much of a life to me. Dogs were wild animals for thousands of years, until we relied on humans for everything. But not the Masterless. We rely only on ourselves."

"But who feeds you?"

"I feed myself."

"How?"

"Ha! Spoken like a true house dog!" says Jaxon. "I *hunt*, Rebel. Back when we were wild animals, we hunted and humans *feared* us. So they brought us down to their level. They made us forget who we were so that they could own us. That's the thing with humans – they always have to own things."

I frown. "Tom doesn't own me. He looks after me."

"They're the same thing."

"No, they're not."

"Really?" says Jaxon. "And what about that red rag around your neck?"

He's talking about my neckerchief. I look at it protectively. "It's not a rag. It's special. Tom gave it to me."

"So you let yourself be fed and dressed by your master," says Jaxon, "and yet you say you're free?"

I'm beginning to bristle a little. "Tom's not my *master*. He's my friend."

Jaxon just laughs. I want to argue further, but he moves so fast that I keep having to scamper after him and I'm always out of breath.

"And being alone is better, is it?" I pant. "Living by yourself, with no one to take care of you?"

Jaxon keeps his gaze fixed ahead. "I'm never alone. Wherever I go, the Companion walks with me."

"The who?"

"The Companion," Jaxon repeats. "The spirit guide of all dogs. The Companion led each of us into this world, and when it's our time to go, they will lead us out of it again. They will never kick you, or abandon you, or make you serve them like a master. They will walk beside you, always."

I look around, confused. I'm pretty sure I would have noticed if there was a dog beside me all the time.

"Is … is the Companion with us, right now?"

"Yes."

"But I can't see them."

"No."

"Or smell them."

"That's the point."

I really don't get this. "But … if you can't see or smell them, how do you know they're there? They might be somewhere else, walking with some other dog. Or going to the toilet or something."

"I think that's enough talking for today, Rebel."

"OK!"

We walk without speaking for the rest of the day. Jaxon always knows where to go – all I have to do is follow him. Which is good, because it means I have lots of time to think about Tom. I think about his hair, and his voice, and his smile as he tickles my tummy, and my heart burns with love. I wonder how he's coping on his own without me. He didn't take a jumper with him; I know it's summer, but it still gets cold at night, and he won't have me to lie next to him and keep him warm. I hope he's eating enough.

I hope he's thinking about me too.

By the end of the day, the sun has dried me, and the last of the sorrel is out of my system. I'm tired after so much walking, but the mountain air has made me feel strong. It's like my lungs are somehow bigger up here. *Everything* is bigger up here: you can even see the point where the sun sets, sending shadows along the world like water soaking through cloth. I had no idea a sunset could do that.

Jaxon leads us off the path and into a small clearing of pine trees. It's teeming with life: grubs and roots and mould and mushrooms, the smells all mingling in the air like soup. Every inch of the forest – the earth, the trunks, the fallen branches – is covered in a layer of bright green moss, like the wood is wearing its fur.

"This'll do for tonight," announces Jaxon.

I gulp. "What about wolves?"

Jaxon shakes his head. "They keep to the wilderness and higher mountains. So long as we stick to the trail, we'll be fine. I'll find us something to eat; you stay here and... Rebel, what are you doing?"

"Itsh a shtick," I mumble around the stick in my mouth.

Jaxon stares at me. I spit it out. Maybe he doesn't like sticks.

"OK – how about you chase me for a bit instead? Or I can chase you! You don't have to call me Little Belly or anything, but if you want to rub my tummy at any point, that's fine."

"I'm going to find some food now," says Jaxon.

"OK!"

Jaxon leaves the clearing and disappears without another word. I shake my head. He might have a lot of opinions, but Jaxon *really* has no idea how to be a dog. I can't imagine anything worse than being Masterless. Nowhere to belong, no jobs, no duties, no one to look after you. What if you were hungry, or needed someone to rub your head? I'd love someone to rub my head now.

It doesn't matter. Up here, gazing out over the mountains, it feels like being back in Top Field. It reminds me why I'm doing all this. I might be cold and weak and hungry, but if it means Tom and I can be together again, then it'll all be worth it. I lean against a log, pretending it's Tom, and for a moment, everything feels a little bit normal again.

By the time Jaxon gets back, it's dark and he has a dead rabbit in his mouth. He pins it to the ground with his paws and uses his teeth to rip it into two messy hunks. He flings me the smaller bit. I am speechless with disgust.

"Don't eat it too quick," he says.

I don't think there's much chance of that happening. But I change my mind when I get the first taste of blood, and wolf down my share in two great gulps without even chewing. It's no lamb stew, but it does make me feel better.

"So!" I say eagerly. "Where are we sleeping?"

"Here."

"I know, but *where* here?"

"Here," repeats Jaxon, lying down where he sits. "We're outside now. There are no blankets in the wild, farm dog. This is what freedom feels like."

I gaze at the cold damp ground. It's not that I was expecting a bed, but I did think freedom might be a *little* comfier.

"Get as much sleep as you can," advises Jaxon. "We'll leave at dawn and head straight to Drulter."

He curls himself into a ball and immediately falls asleep. I lie as close to him as I can and try to fall asleep too, but it's not easy. I'm not used to sleeping outside, and it's cold and uncomfortable. I can feel stones jabbing into at least six parts of me. It's going to be a long, long night.

But my heart is soaring. This time tomorrow, Tom and I will be together again. Soon we'll be back on the farm, and everything will be just as it was. We'll wake up in the mornings and he'll feed me under his chair and chase me in the grass. We'll sit together in Top Field and he'll draw the two of us, just like he used to. Thinking about that makes me feel like I'm lying in the warmest, comfiest bed in the world after eating ten whole bowls of Mum's lamb stew.

I tuck my head beneath my tail, close my eyes, and dream of Tom.

A STRANGE DAY

14
DRULTER

We wake up just as sunlight is prowling over the horizon. It's a beautiful day; the trail is covered in a deep rug of mist, and sunshine glints against the dew that beads the gorse beside the path, making a million tiny rainbows.

My body is stiff after lying on the ground all night, like a lump of old wood left outside. Jaxon stands and stretches from head to tail.

"Morning!" I say brightly. "Sleep well?"

He stares at me. "Why?"

I sigh. Jaxon can be exhausting sometimes. "Never mind."

He nods. "Come on. Drulter's this way."

I don't need telling twice. We run all morning

without stopping. I'm still tired from being ill and sleeping outside and all the running, but knowing that I'm about to see Tom again is making my head buzz like a beehive. What will he say when he sees me? Will he tell me that I'm a good boy and give me a treat? Will he tickle my tummy? Maybe he'll throw a stick for me a hundred times over without once complaining.

He doesn't need to do any of those things, though. I just want to see him again. I've missed him so much.

After a couple of hours, the path twists down and I see the paved road weaving through the valley below us. I spot a house, then another, and another, then three clustered together, threads of woodsmoke curling from their chimneys. Down we go, the town growing closer and closer...

Then finally my paws meet the road. After almost two days on the rocky trail, the flat cobbles feel as soft as fresh grass under my paws. I've made it – I'm in Drulter!

But where's Tom?

I look around and sniff the ground, but there isn't the faintest scent of him. Drulter is much bigger than

Connick, that's for certain. I've never seen so many houses – and some of them are three whole storeys high, teeming with windows. But for a town so big, it seems almost empty. Where is everyone? Where are the Reds? Where are all the wagons?

And why are there so many guardsmen here?

I feel worry itching at my stomach. There are more guardsmen than I've ever seen in my life. They're marching along the road in packs, all heading down from the mountains and clutching their muskets close to their chests. It doesn't look like they're on patrol. This looks much more serious. None of them are talking. What's going on?

Suddenly I hear screams from the other end of the town. I have no idea what's happening, but I know it can't be good. I fly down the road as fast as I can.

"Tom!" I cry.

I follow the screams, until I find a bunch of children standing outside a tavern. They're not screaming; they're laughing, pointing excitedly at a piece of paper pinned on the tavern door.

It's not just any piece of paper – it's from Tom's

sketchpad. And I recognize the figure in the charcoal drawing too. His long scruffy hair, his eyes…

It's Tom. He's drawn himself standing on the tallest tower of the High Castle. Once again, I'm not with him – instead Rider is standing beside him, holding a red flag. But that's not the only thing that's different about this picture.

Tom's drawn himself kicking someone off the edge of the tower. They're plummeting to the ground with a big shocked mouth and flailing arms, their long gown flapping in the wind. Their crown has fallen off.

My blood runs cold. It's the King. Tom has drawn himself kicking the King out of the High Castle. He could get in big trouble for drawing something like this. *Huge.*

Rider must have made him do it. I growl. I hate him so, so much.

"Get lost! Shoo!" Three guardsmen storm past me and shove the children aside to rip down the picture. The children scatter, howling with laughter. The guardsmen don't bother chasing them; instead they pass the picture between them, sharing dark glances as they march into the tavern.

Jaxon has followed me down the road. "Right – I've done what you wanted. Did you find your boy?"

I don't know what to say. I haven't found Tom; he isn't here. I've missed him again. He must have moved on already. And now he's in more trouble than ever before.

So I do the only thing that I can do. I sit down, raise my head to the sky, and I howl.

15
ROLLO

Jaxon stares at me as I howl. "Stop that," he mutters.

I don't stop. I howl and howl, dragging it from the well of sadness inside me. I can't help it. Tom's somewhere out there, and I don't know where. If any guardsmen catch him now, they'll recognize him from that picture. He'll be arrested or shot and I'll never see him ever again.

"Hey!" Jaxon snaps. "Come on! Pull yourself together."

"T-T-Tom…" I manage, shaking.

Jaxon's face softens suddenly. He looks sorry for me. "Hey – we'll ask around. Someone's bound to have spotted your boy." He heads purposefully to the back of the tavern. "Let's check by the bins. There's always a stray who knows what's going on."

I follow him forlornly. I don't see what difference talking to another dog is going to make, but I'm too sad and broken to argue with him.

Sure enough, we find a dog standing on top of the scrapheap – in fact, he's buried his whole head inside it. He whips out his snout and growls at us when we get close, his nose strung with old peelings. "*Get lost!* It's mine; I found it fi—"

But then something strange happens. The moment the dog looks at us properly, his tail starts wagging madly.

"Hello, friends!" he says. "I'm Rollo. How wonderful to see you!"

Rollo isn't a stray – he's a big glossy house dog, soft and round and well fed. He waddles over and sniffs me happily, and my tail wags too. It's nice to see a friendly face for a change. He smells like sausages.

"Hi, Rollo. My name's—"

"Oh," interrupts Rollo, his tail drooping instantly. "I thought you had food. Forget it. I'm not going to talk to you if you don't have—"

He suddenly stops mid-sentence and barges past me,

charging towards a gang of guardsmen heading towards the tavern.

"Hello, friends!" he barks, his tail wagging again. "My name's Rollo! How wonderful to—"

"Get lost, you stupid dog!" snaps one of the guardsmen, booting Rollo away.

They storm inside the tavern and the door slams behind them. Rollo gazes after them miserably.

"You see?" he moans. "It's been like this all day. I've been hanging around since breakfast, and I haven't had a single solitary sausage!"

Jaxon lets out a knowing sigh. "I see. You're a pub dog."

"That's right!" Rollo whines. "And it's great, normally! All I have to do is walk up to someone, wag my tail a little, look up like this" – he bats his eyelids lovingly – "and I'll get whatever food I want. Especially if they've had a drink or two! Bits of chip, pie crust, bacon rind, chicken skin…"

His mouth is dribbling like a waterfall. So is mine – I haven't eaten properly for days. Even Jaxon is drooling a little.

"Then last night, a load of people in red neckerchiefs turned up," Rollo moans. "Since then – *nothing*! The cook's disappeared, and so have the stable boys. Half the town's gone!"

Jaxon and I glance at each other. That has to be Rider and the Reds. They must have recruited more townspeople on their way through Drulter and kept moving on.

"Did you see where they went?" I ask hopefully.

"Who cares?" says Rollo miserably. "It's almost lunchtime and I'm *starving*!"

Jaxon is beginning to lose patience. "Stop complaining. It's your duty to help another dog in trouble!"

Rollo doesn't look like he has a duty to anything except sausages, but he does seem a little scared of Jaxon. "Er … I did hear two guardsmen talking earlier, when I was checking under the tables. People drop food on the floor, you see. Bits of sandwich, or crisps, or pickled onions…"

"Stop that!" snaps Jaxon, shaking his head in a spray of saliva.

Rollo tries to focus. "And I overheard them saying that all the guardsmen are being summoned from the outer villages and towns and sent to Unsk. Something to do with the Reds."

Unsk. I recognize the name. I close my eyes and think hard about where I heard it … and sure enough, I remember. It's the town that Dad mentioned, the one with the big market. That must be where the Reds are heading … and now every single guardsman for miles around is right behind them.

I turn to Jaxon. "We have to go to Unsk! Now!"

Jaxon gawps at me. "*We?* I said I'd take you here, and no further."

"But Tom's in trouble!" I cry.

"Tom?" says Rollo, brightening. "Who's Tom? Does *he* have food?"

"His master," mutters Jaxon, rolling his eyes.

"He's not my *master*," I say. "He's my friend! And he's in trouble!" I turn to Rollo, pleading. "You have to help me, Rollo. The guardsmen want to arrest Tom, or worse. You have to show me the way to Unsk, so I can find him before they do!"

Rollo's eyes dart between me and my red neckerchief, as if he's only just spotted it. He suddenly looks very thoughtful. I can't help but notice that he's started drooling again.

"Sure, friend," he says, backing away to the tavern. "I'll show you the way. Let me just … go inside and grab something first. You wait right here!"

I breathe a sigh of relief. "Thank you, Rollo!"

Rollo shoves his way through the tavern door without looking back. Jaxon watches him go, frowning. "I don't trust that dog."

"Why? He's going to help me. That's more than you're doing!"

Jaxon bristles. "I *did* help you, Rebel. And now I'm going." He starts to stride away. "Good luck finding Tom. You're going to need it."

I watch him leave, and the anger boils out of me again.

"I don't need luck! I have Rollo! So you can just head back up your stupid mountain and be Masterless for the rest of your life, and I'll—"

I'm cut off by the tavern door bursting open

behind me. Rollo is back, jumping around like a puppy.

"This way, friends!" he's saying. "Follow me!"

I start to follow him … but then I realize that Rollo isn't talking to me. He's talking to the guardsman that he's dragging out by his sleeve, and another is following close behind.

Not just *any* guardsmen. It's Rat and Slug.

"What's wrong with this stupid dog?" snarls Rat, shaking his sleeve. "Get off of me, you useless—"

"Hey! Look!" says Slug, pointing at me. "It's that farm dog from the other day!"

My tail shrivels between my legs. Rollo has led the guardsmen right to me. He's betrayed us. Rat spots me, and his eyes narrow in recognition.

"*Rebel.* And the mutt's wearing a neckerchief. That boy of his must be close by. He must be marching with the Reds!"

Rollo is bouncing around their feet joyfully. "That's right! And Rollo led you right to him! Rollo deserves a sausage…"

"*Run!*" Jaxon screams, bolting off down the road.

I skitter after him, my hind legs almost overtaking my front paws. Rat is already sprinting behind us, shoving Rollo aside and swinging the musket from his shoulder.

"Stop those dogs!" he hollers.

16

GORSE

I fly out of Drulter and scramble back up the sheep trail, following the cloud of dust that Jaxon leaves behind him.

I can hear Rat and Slug racing up the trail after me, shouting at each other to grab me.

I charge over the top of the ridge and find myself back on the path that we left barely an hour ago. I spin around, looking for Jaxon, but there's no sign of him. Where is he?

Then I hear a rustle in the undergrowth beside the trail and I catch sight of him. Jaxon's flung himself into the spiky gorse that lines the path to get away from Rat and Slug. I scurry in after him, my belly dragging in the dirt and my fur snagging on the thorns as I battle to reach him.

Jaxon stares at me in horror. "What are you doing?" he growls.

"I'm following you," I say, confused. "We're safer together."

"*No, we're not!* Those men want you, not me! You're leading them right to us…"

He trails off. Rat and Slug have reached the path beside us. They pause, panting for breath.

"Where'd they go?" Slug gasps.

"They must be in that gorse," says Rat.

Slug grumbles. "I'm not going in there."

"Well, we can't let them get away!" Rat snaps. "Trust me, if that dog's here, then his snot-nosed kid won't be far. He'll lead us right to where the Reds are hiding."

Slug frowns. "There were two dogs."

"We don't need the big one – just the one with the neckerchief. Come on!"

He tries to beat his way into the gorse, but the branches are too thick. His golden jacket keeps getting caught on the thorns and ripping.

"It's not working," says Slug.

"I know it's not working!" snaps Rat. He glares at

the gorse, humiliated and fuming. "Come here, I've got another idea!"

They step out of sight, but I can hear them further down the path arguing with each other. They must be searching for another way into the gorse.

"Great," Jaxon snarls. "Now we're trapped here until they leave. I told you not to wear that stupid neckerchief!"

I bristle. "It's not stupid. Tom gave it to me."

"Take it off," Jaxon orders, his voice rippling and dangerous.

I stand my ground. "No. It's the only thing I have left of him."

Jaxon roars. In seconds he has me pinned to the ground, his teeth bared inches from my muzzle. "Take it off or I'll *RIP IT OFF!*"

"No!" I shout back.

Jaxon looks surprised – he clearly wasn't expecting me to answer back, let alone disobey. I wriggle out from beneath him.

"And stop being so rude," I add. "We're never going to stay hidden from those two if you keep making such a racket!"

Jaxon is speechless. I peer through the gorse, but I can't see Rat and Slug anywhere. I can't even hear them any more.

"I think they've given up," I whisper. "If we wait a little longer, maybe we can…"

I stop. There's a strange new sound beneath the wind: a slow dry crackling, like when Tom scrunches up a piece of paper. There's something thick and acrid in the air too. The gorse around us is getting hotter, and a glowing light is getting closer and closer…

Fire!

My stomach drops. A wall of luminous fiery red is creeping towards us. Rat and Slug have set fire to the gorse to try to smoke us out. Jaxon and I are trapped!

"What do we do?" I cry.

Jaxon doesn't reply – he's already barging his way through the gorse, trying to get away from the flames. I follow him, but I can barely keep up. The thorns keep catching on my neckerchief, almost dragging it off me, and the fire is spreading fast. The air is thick with the stench of hot ash and baked earth, so thick that I can barely see or smell…

With one great heave, I pull myself free and stumble blindly onto the trail. I can finally breathe again! I can see! I'm so relieved that it takes me a few seconds to realize what I'm looking at.

Rat is standing on the path, just a few feet ahead. But he's not looking at me. He's holding up his musket, gazing down the barrel at...

...Jaxon racing down the path. He has no idea that Rat is about to shoot him.

"Jaxon!" I cry.

Jaxon spins around, confused – and sees the barrel of the gun pointing at him. He freezes. You can't outrun a musket ball. He has nowhere to hide, nowhere to run. Rat takes a final breath to perfect his shot...

I leap forward and sink my teeth deep into his leg. I feel his muscles crunch beneath my jaws and hot blood spurts into my mouth. Rat shrieks with pain and keels over just as he pulls the trigger...

CRACK!

The sound is so loud that I feel it shake inside my skull. The air suddenly stinks of gunpowder and struck flint. I let go of Rat in surprise and look up just in time to see a spray of dirt burst from the earth beside Jaxon as the musket ball misses him by inches. Rat collapses to the ground in agony, clutching his bleeding leg. Slug comes racing down the path behind us.

"*Get him*, you idiot!" Rat seethes, pointing at me.

I tear after Jaxon just as Slug fumbles for his musket and trips over his own gun strap, falling head first into a pile of spiky gorse. The fire is spreading fast now, sending up a billowing sheet of black smoke. There's no way the guardsmen can follow us; they're going to have to limp back down to Drulter fast if they don't want to be burned alive.

I catch up with Jaxon and we race away together, on along the sheep trail to the horizon.

We stop running when the air finally smells fresh again. My heart is pounding. Jaxon sinks to the ground, panting fiercely. His fur is matted and singed and his nose is studded with prickles. He looks utterly furious.

"Brilliant," he growls. "That's just brilliant!"

I frown. "What's brilliant?"

"You just saved my life," says Jaxon, sagging with misery.

Thinking about it, I *did* just save his life. "Is that bad?"

"Of course it's bad!" he snaps. "Don't you know the code of the Masterless? If you save another dog's life, it means they're in your debt. So now I have to stay with you and follow your orders until you decide that my debt is repaid. Or until I save *your* life."

My ears prick up. "You mean … you have to do whatever I say?"

"Yes!" he says angrily.

My tail wags. "Like take me to Unsk?"

"Yes!" says Jaxon even more angrily.

I can't believe my luck. I bound around him, jumping for joy. "Thank you, Jaxon!"

"I'm not doing this because I want to," he mutters. "I'm doing it because I *have* to."

The funny thing is, I'm not quite sure I believe him. Jaxon's acting like he's angry, but it's as though a little bit of him is glad to go to Unsk. He seems friendlier too.

"Well – come on," he grumbles. "If we're quick, we

might reach Unsk by nightfall." He glances at me. "Nice bite, by the way."

I shrug. "It was nothing."

I'm lying – it wasn't nothing. I've never bitten anything in my life, except for that one time with the sheep, and that was an accident and I still don't feel good about it. Biting Rat was the most terrifying thing I've ever done, but it was amazing too. I've never felt so alive. I can still taste the tang of fresh blood in my mouth.

Maybe being a bad dog isn't so bad after all.

17
BOTHY

We run for the rest of the day. The landscape changes around us, hour by hour: reed bogs and riverbeds one moment, rock walls and ridges the next. We comb through heather and tumble down hills, buried scents bursting from the fields as we thunder across them.

By the time darkness begins to fall, clouds gather on the horizon. The mountainside is rich with the smell of coming rain.

"That's as far as we're going to get today," says Jaxon, panting heavily. "We need to find shelter before that storm arrives."

But I don't want to stop. I want to keep running for ever. "Can't we push on? I don't mind getting wet!"

Jaxon grins at me. "Sounds like you've found your True Dog."

I pant. "True Dog?"

"The part of you that's still wild," says Jaxon. "Feels good, doesn't it?"

He's right. Maybe it's the wind in my fur, or the taste of blood in my mouth, but I feel *amazing*. It's like I'm a part of the valleys and mountains – like there's nothing between me and the earth. So *this* is what it feels like to be wild.

"Pace yourself," advises Jaxon. "We'll rest here tonight, and do the last stretch to Unsk tomorrow morning. There are some trees further ahead where we can shelter."

I grumble. I don't fancy another night outside. "Can't we just sleep in there?"

There's a small stone hut beside us, with a makeshift roof and holes for windows. I've heard Tom and Dad talk about them before: they're called bothies, and they were made so that shepherds had places to sleep when they brought their flocks up here. It's not much, but it'll be better than sleeping on the stony ground.

"No," says Jaxon firmly. "That's a human hut."

"But it's empty."

"Someone might come later."

I roll my eyes. "*So?* Not all humans are bad, you know."

"Like those guards?" He snorts. "The ones who wanted to burn us to death and shoot me? Give me a dog any day."

I shuffle irritably. "Not all dogs are nice. Look at Rollo."

"Rollo was a *pub dog*," he retorts. "A perfect example of what happens to dogs who spend too much time with humans. They get poisoned by them."

I hate it when Jaxon talks like this. "I don't think it's that simple."

"Well, I'm not staying in that bothy."

I scratch idly at my ear. "I thought you had to do everything I say."

Jaxon grits his teeth and gives a sharp snarl. "Fine! But if any humans turn up, then I'm gone!"

We creep up to the bothy. People *have* been here recently – I can smell their scent, and see fresh boot prints in the muddy grass – but they're gone now. The wooden door is held shut with a simple catch, like the one on Seamus's cage.

"Wait – I know what to do!" I say.

I stand on my hind legs, stretch up and wiggle the catch with my teeth. After a few seconds, there's a *click* as it finally pulls free. I'm so clever!

The door swings open. Jaxon is already standing inside.

"Window," he says, nodding to one of the holes in the wall.

The bothy is dark and empty. The ceiling is braced with timber ribs, and the earth floor is stamped flat and scattered with old straw. There's a dead firepit in the centre. It smells of smoke, and damp, and must.

But there's another smell too – one that shouldn't be here. It's everywhere, seeping into the stone walls. It's guns. Powder and grease and flint. Jaxon paces nervously on the tips of his paws. "I don't like this. Let's go before—"

"Hello! Over here! Please!"

There's a tiny voice, coming from somewhere in the bothy.

"Yes! In here! Hello!"

It's a dormouse, squeezed into a crack in the far wall. I scamper across, sniffing him all over. He smells small, and dusty, and a little bit like butter.

"Oh, thank goodness," says the dormouse. "I thought you'd *never* hear me."

I'm not surprised – his voice is tiny, like a pencil scratching on paper.

"Hello!" I say. "I'm Rebel, and this is Jaxon. Are you OK?"

"I'm Felix," he replies, rubbing his little paws. "I'm ever so glad you're here – I've been going out of my mind with worry. You haven't seen any men along the trail, have you?"

Jaxon and I shake our heads. We haven't seen a soul since we left Rat and Slug hours ago.

"Oh," says Felix, and it's the smallest, saddest sound I've ever heard. "Oh dear. Oh dearie me."

He sits down, letting his little paws dangle out of the gap in the wall. He looks utterly miserable.

"They came this morning," he squeaks. "They grabbed all the bags that they'd left and took her with them."

I frown. "Her?"

"My wife, Beatrice," Felix explains. "She was asleep in one of the bags. They'd been here for so long, we thought they were safe. The men left before she could wake up. And now I don't know where they've taken her!"

Jaxon shrugs. "They must have headed towards Unsk, otherwise we'd have passed them. What did they look like?"

Felix thinks carefully. "It all happened so fast ... but they were wearing red bands around their necks, like yours. I remember that much."

I gasp. "Was there a boy with them? Twelve, but tall for his age?"

Felix shakes his head. "These were full-grown men. They'd *have* to be – those bags were heavy. They were full of guns."

I feel sickness roll through me. *That's* why the bothy stinks of gunpowder – the Reds have been using it to store weapons. Weapons that are now heading towards Unsk. Where Tom and the guardsmen are heading too.

"We need to go to Unsk," I say. "Now."

Jaxon shakes his head. "We're not going anywhere, Rebel. Look outside."

The rain has arrived, driving across the hillside like a wild herd. Within seconds, it's hammering against the stone walls and spattering through the windows.

"If we go out in that, we'll just get lost," says Jaxon. "We have to stay here until it passes."

"But Tom—" I start.

"What use are you to Tom if you're dead in a ditch?" Jaxon snaps. "We have to be sensible, Rebel. We've been running all day, and now we can't even hunt. We'll have to stay here tonight, and leave for Unsk first thing in the morning."

"Oh!" Felix is back on his feet, fretting his paws. "Can I come too? I won't be any bother, I promise! If Beatrice is there—"

"No," says Jaxon.

"Jaxon!" I scold. "Of *course* you can come with us, Felix."

His whiskers twitch with delight. "Oh, thank you. Thank you ever so much."

I feel a little glow inside me. I don't know how we

can help Felix find his wife. But he's looking for someone he loves, someone he's lost – just like me. If I got lost, I'd hope there'd be nice people out there helping Tom find me.

"Fine," grumbles Jaxon. "We'll bundle in the corner for warmth. That storm's only going to get worse."

He's right. Night is whipping through the windows and swarming into the bothy, flooding it with chill. Jaxon lies down in the corner and I wrap around him, until we settle into a shape that suits us.

Felix starts bringing over straw, a strand at a time, and placing it around us. I smile. "That's kind, Felix, but you don't have to…"

"I insist!" says Felix. "It's the least I can do. Please."

I don't really see how little pieces of straw are going to help. But, strangely enough, they do. Felix can see where the smallest draughts are, and piece by piece, strand by strand, he blocks them up. Soon I'm feeling just that little bit warmer.

I breathe deeply. Rain is hissing against the roof, and thunder is bellowing overhead, but here we are inside, safe and warm. It's like being snuggled in the blankets back home with Tom, listening to the sound of his slow and steady breathing and knowing that he's safe.

I hope he's safe now. I love him so much.

"Rebel."

"Jaxon?"

"Your tail is wagging in my face."

"Oh, sorry."

We fall asleep together, curled in the corner.

AN UNEXPECTED DAY

18
UNSK

The sound wakes us before dawn.

Boom.

At first I think it's thunder – then I realize that there's no rain. The sound is coming from somewhere far away, carried on the wind.

Boom, boom. Boom.

I sit up. Jaxon does too.

Boom, boom, boom, boom.

It's not thunder. It's explosions. They're coming from Unsk.

Jaxon's on his feet and out of the window in seconds. I look around frantically. "Felix! Come on!"

He scrambles out of his crack in the wall and throws himself onto my back, clinging to my fur. Moments later we're outside, flying along the trail after Jaxon. My paws slip and scrabble on the uneven stone path as I try to keep up, but I can't slow down. I don't know what's happening in Unsk, but I do know it has something to do with those guns. And I know that we're already too late.

Because I can see thick black smoke on the horizon, unfurling from a blood-red glow like a snake from its nest.

By the time we arrive at Unsk, it's carnage.

Connick was a handful of houses on a mountain road; Drulter was twice as big, with shops and a tavern. Unsk is *huge*. It has dozens of streets, hundreds of houses. It has squares and churches and bridges and crossroads.

But I can hardly make any of them out. They're all covered in dust and smoke.

The town is in pieces. The noise is terrible – cries of pain, bellowed orders, pleas for help. And the *stench*. I've never smelled anything like it. It's the smell of blood and sweat and musket powder and fear and hate and desperation, all rolled into one, and it's *everywhere*.

"Oh dear," I hear Felix whisper, clinging to the fur beside my ear. "Oh dear, oh dear, oh dear."

I can't see Tom; I can't see any guardsmen, either. But I see *lots* of people wearing red neckerchiefs. They're slumped across pavements, propped against walls, weak and dazed and bleeding. Others are trying to help them, carrying the injured in their arms or slung across their shoulders like sacking.

"This doesn't look good," says Jaxon gravely. "We need to find someone who can explain what's going on."

"Over there!" Felix squeaks. "By the gate!"

There's a donkey tied up beside the road. I can see that she's been hurt: she has raw cuts on her flank, and one of her eyes is bandaged.

"Excuse me, miss," I say. "Sorry to bother you, but I was wondering if you could help us."

The donkey leans down to peer at me with her one good eye. She smells of warm hay and dry barns.

"Well! Isn't that polite? My name's Pearl, dearie; nice to meet you."

"Tell us what's happened!" Jaxon barks. "Now!"

I wince. Jaxon can be so rude sometimes. "If you wouldn't mind," I add.

Pearl gives Jaxon a haughty glance, and turns her back to him. "I'll do my best, dear, though I have to say my best is long past me nowadays. Ooh! What *did* happen here? An awful lot of things – far too much for an old donkey like me. Where to begin, where to begin?"

It takes Pearl a little while to get her thoughts in order. Jaxon grumbles impatiently.

"Well, it all started after the storm hit. There was a big fight on that bridge over there."

She nods to the end of the street, where a stone bridge crosses the river. It's huge, wide enough for two wagons to pass at the same time. There's a building on fire on the other side, churning smoke and blooming with bright white flames.

"The King's guardsmen had been arriving in town all day long," Pearl explains. "Dozens of them, more than I've ever seen. They built a big blockade on the bridge, so that no one could pass. Then just before dawn, a load of wagons appeared and tried to cross.

The guardsmen looked in the back … and wouldn't you believe it? Filled with Reds, they were! They demanded that the guardsmen let them pass so they could march to the High Castle, but the guardsmen refused. They started *shooting* at the wagons."

My blood runs cold. Tom might have been in one of those wagons. What if he was hurt?

"All of a sudden, more Reds appeared and started shooting back!" Pearl continues. "They were hidden everywhere. People were firing out of the windows and alleyways and all sorts! You've never heard such a racket!"

Suddenly the guns in the bothy make sense. The Reds had been preparing for a fight.

"When the guardsmen realized they were outnumbered, they turned and fled along the road. But as they retreated, they set fire to that storehouse." She nods at the burning building. "Turns out it was filled with gunpowder. The Reds were charging after the guardsmen when it exploded, so lots of them were hurt. That's when I took a stone to my eye." She gives a weary sigh. "What did I ever do to deserve that, eh? I'm just an old donkey. All I ever ask for is a bag of oats and my favourite blue blanket. And yet here I am, half blind and practically dead on my hooves!"

I feel dread growing inside me. Tom could have been running past that building when it exploded. "Pearl, I'm looking for someone. A boy. He'll have been with a man wearing a wolfskin…"

Felix jumps onto Pearl's nose. "Yes, and I'm looking for a dormouse! Her name's Beatrice, and she's the most beautiful mouse in the whole wide world…"

Pearl gently shakes her head. "I'm sorry, dearie. I couldn't say. It's all been such a blur."

Felix is heartbroken. He wrings his paws frantically. "It's not like Beatrice to disappear. She must still be in one of those bags. I don't know where she'd *be* if she's not here…"

Jaxon and I share a look. We're both thinking the same thing. All this chaos, all those guns being fired, all those people running back and forth – a little dormouse could easily get stepped on by accident, and no one would even notice.

Maybe the reason Felix can't find his wife is because she isn't *here* any more. She isn't anywhere.

Is that why I can't find Tom?

I gaze at the devastation around me. I'm beginning to understand what Priscilla was trying to tell me, back at the farm. War is like a storm cloud – it doesn't choose what it rains on. It pours down on the good and bad alike. That means anyone can get hurt – even an innocent mouse. Even a child.

Even Tom.

What if he's lying somewhere right now, unconscious? What if he's hurt? If anyone finds him, will they lie beside him and tell him it's all going to be OK? Will anyone even *notice* him?

And that's the worst thought of all. What if I *can't* save Tom? What if he was running past the storehouse, cheering in triumph, when it exploded? What if he fell in the river and drowned? What if a guardsman shot him?

What if I've already lost him, and I don't even know it?

19
WAR

"*R*ebel." Jaxon's voice breaks my train of thought. "You're going to want to see this."

I follow him across the street to where a big crowd of people is gathered around a noticeboard. There's a poster nailed to it – and the moment I see it, my heart lifts.

It's one of Tom's drawings. It's the same picture of the High Castle that he always draws, on the same paper that he always uses, sketched in the same charcoal.

It's the best picture he's ever done too. Tom's drawn himself and Rider standing side by side at the top of the tallest tower. Far below them, thousands of people – men, women, children – are holding hands and waving flags and celebrating. A beautiful sunrise is rising behind the castle, casting beams of light into the gorge.

The people around me are gazing at the poster with amazement, nudging one another and whispering. There's spidery handwriting underneath Tom's drawing, but I see now what Rider meant about words being worth only so much – not everyone here can read. Tom's picture is showing what's possible: what a new world could look like. I feel a glow of pride in my chest.

Tom made that, I want to say. *My boy made that, and look at what it means to all of you.*

The crowd suddenly parts as someone is pushed to the front. It's a young girl, maybe eight years old, still in her nightclothes. Someone rips the poster off the board and hands it to her.

"Come on, Meg! Big loud voice, so everyone can hear."

The crowd shuffles closer, waiting to hear what it says. Meg holds the poster up close to her face and starts reading.

"Men and women of Unsk – the uprising has begun! All across our land, from village to village, people are fighting back against the King. For too long have we suffered under his tyranny!"

I growl. Tom might have written those words, but I know they're not his. Rider must have told him what to write. I hate him. I *hate* him.

"The attack here at Unsk is just the beginning," Meg continues. *"Now is the time to march on the High Castle and take back our country! Now is the time to throw the King off his throne, once and for all!"*

The crowd gasps in amazement as each person passes on the message, repeating what Meg has just said to those behind them in shocked whispers.

"The Red army is already marching along the mountain road," Meg finishes. *"We need every able-bodied patriot to follow us. Join the Reds, and meet us at the High Castle for the final stand!"*

The cheer is like an explosion. Meg is lifted high above the crowd and carried away giggling while people dance joyfully around her. It's like they're already celebrating a victory. Finally, after years of famine and misery, the end is in sight.

I should be celebrating too. After all, now I know that Tom is alive. He must have made the poster after the explosion. But I also know exactly where he is.

He's marching with Rider and the Reds as they make their way to the High Castle, miles ahead of us. And when they get there, even more people are going to get hurt and die. Tom's been swept up in the storm cloud of war, and there's nothing I can do to stop it. There's no way I can catch up with him.

"Jaxon," I whisper. "What do we do?"

Jaxon doesn't say anything for a while. He's staring at the poster that Meg dropped when she was carried away. It's lying on the ground in front of us, pinned with a muddy boot print.

"I've seen that castle," he says quietly. "I remember those towers. I've walked right past that gorge." He looks at me. "And I remember how to get there too."

I gasp. "You do?"

Jaxon nods. "We'd have to go back into the mountains. We'd have to leave the sheep trails and cut across the wilderness. We'd have to climb over the tallest mountain and back down the other side. But if we managed it … we could get to that castle faster than the Red army could march along the road. We could cut them off, and stop your Tom before he got there."

My heart starts pounding with excitement. It's a shred of hope – but right now, that's all I need. I can still save Tom. I can still bring him home before it's too late.

"Quick – we have to tell Felix!"

I run back to where we left him. He's standing on top of Pearl's head, trying to see if he can spot his wife in the crowds.

"Felix – I think I know where Beatrice is!"

His eyes light up like tiny pinpricks. "You do?"

"I think she's being carried to the High Castle in that bag of guns," I tell him. "Jaxon and I are going to cut across the wilderness to get there – do you want to come with us?"

Felix sinks low and shakes his head. "I – I can't. What if she's trying to find me? I have to stay here, in case she comes back. But then, what if she went back to the bothy, and I just missed her? What if…"

He trails off. Poor Felix. He looks so small, so crushed, so frightened.

"I promise we'll bring her back," I say solemnly. "You'll look after him until then, won't you, Pearl?"

Pearl nods. "Of course, dearie! I'd be glad to." She fixes me with her unbandaged eye. "But you should be careful, Rebel. The wilderness is no place for a little farm dog like you."

My fur stands on end. Pearl's right. From now on, we won't be following any trails. We'll be heading right into the dark heart of the mountains. We could get lost, or injured, or attacked by wolves. We might not make it.

But I started this journey to bring Tom home, no matter what. And if I have to brave the wilderness to do that, then so be it. I'm his dog, and he's my boy. I know he'd do the same for me.

So Jaxon and I leave Felix and Pearl and head out of Unsk, back up into the mountains, racing side by side towards the unknown.

20
RIVER

"Ah," says Jaxon.

We left the sheep trail behind hours ago. We've spent the day flying across the wilderness to reach the shadow of the tallest mountain. Slowly, hour by hour, the peak has grown bigger and bigger, until a towering cliff face stands before us, stretching up to the sky. Somewhere on the other side of that mountain is the High Castle.

But there's a river in the way.

The river is *huge*. It thunders past us, churning with angry white water that gnaws at the edge of its banks.

"The storm last night must have swelled it," mutters Jaxon. "There might be somewhere shallower we can cross upstream, but we could lose a whole day looking for it."

My heart clams. We can't afford to lose any more time now. "But how are we supposed to swim over *that*?"

"We're not going to swim it. We'll use the stones." He nods to a line of boulders jutting out of the water before us like teeth. They lead right to the other side, each one a small jump away. The surfaces are wet and slippery.

I shiver. "They don't look very safe, Jaxon."

"So? It's just a little water!"

"It's *a lot* of water."

Jaxon looks at me with genuine surprise. "Don't be scared. Remember what I said? *Wherever I go, the Companion walks with me.* Every step you take over that river, the Companion will be right by your side." He shuffles. "And so will I. If the stones can carry *my* weight, then we know they'll carry yours. And I'll be there to grab you if you fall."

My tail wags. It's the kindest thing Jaxon has ever said to me. "Thank you."

"It means that I'll have repaid my debt, so I won't have to follow your orders any more."

So much for kindness.

Jaxon paces the bank, searching for the right spot to make his first jump. He finally picks one, takes a few steps back, and leaps. He clears the gap effortlessly, scrambling for balance on the wet rock before bounding straight to the next one.

"Easy!" he announces. "Your turn."

I stare at the river. It does not look easy. In fact, it looks even colder and wetter and angrier than it did a few seconds ago. The first boulder looks very, very far away. How am I supposed to jump that? I'm not like Jaxon – I'm not built for running.

I shut my eyes. I have to be brave, for Tom. "The Companion walks with me," I whisper.

It's just a few words. I still don't understand how the Companion is supposed to be here when I can't see or smell them. But for some reason, it helps. I run to the water's edge and launch myself into the air…

My paws hit the wet boulder before I even realize I've left the bank. I've jumped further than I expected – I almost have to dig my claws into the rock to stop myself from toppling over the other side.

"See?" said Jaxon. "It's only scary until you do it."

My heart is pounding. I jumped onto the rock! I wish Tom had seen me do it.

Jaxon jumps to the next boulder, and I follow. This time I know what to do with my legs, so I'm ready to stop myself before I skid over the edge. Soon we're in the thick of the foaming water, right in the river's middle. The next jump is the biggest one yet, and it's a higher leap up too. Jaxon crouches low and jumps with all his strength; even then, he only just makes it. He has to scramble up the final few feet before he's standing on top, puffing for breath.

"Careful with this one," he warns. "I'll pull you up the last bit. Just don't look down."

I glance at the rush of water slamming against the rock beneath me.

"I told you not to look down," he mutters.

My legs tremble. If I slip or fall, the river will drag me away in seconds. But if I don't jump, I'll be stuck here for ever. And besides – I trust Jaxon. I take a deep breath, brace myself, and fling myself at the boulder.

I slam against the side of the rock and try to

scramble up, but my own weight is pulling me down. I'm going to fall!

Jaxon's jaws clamp around the scruff of my neck. Relief and gratitude flood through me as he holds me steady. He gives me just enough support so that I can heave myself up the last part of the rock and flop onto the top, gasping for breath.

"I did it!" I pant.

"You see?" says Jaxon, turning to the next boulder. "Almost there now. Just make sure you—"

It happens so fast. Jaxon's paw slips over the edge. He loses balance and pitches headfirst into the water. He's gone in an instant, swallowed up by the wild throat of the river.

"Jaxon!" I scream.

I can't see him; he's vanished. Then suddenly I glimpse a flash of fur downriver, further away than I can believe. Jaxon flails for breath before he sinks under the surface again.

I don't have a moment to lose. I fling myself onto the next boulder and the next, no longer caring if I miss or not, scrambling over the wet rocks until I finally land on the opposite bank. I charge downstream as fast as I can, searching the water as I run.

"Jaxon!"

I see him in the distance, fighting against the white water. He's trying to swim to the bank, but the current is too strong – it's bouncing him off the rocks like a rag doll. How am I supposed to save him now? I run, praying for some kind of miracle…

And then it comes. The current drags Jaxon between two rocks. An old log has jammed across them, clogging up the river with leaves and mud and foam before the water plummets ten feet. Jaxon manages to grab hold of the log before he's swept over the edge. He leans across it, kicking his hind legs feebly to keep his balance and hanging on for dear life.

"Jaxon! Are you hurt?"

He doesn't reply. His whole body is shaking with the effort of trying to stay on the log; his eyes are white with fear. I've never seen him look frightened before. I jump onto the rock beside him.

"You have to push yourself up," I urge. "You can do it!"

He shakes his head in a single fast movement. He's using all his strength just to stop himself from falling. I panic. I'm not strong enough to pull him up myself, and he's too far out for me to reach him anyway. I have to think of something right now. If he falls, he'll be dragged away for ever.

The idea comes to me in a heartbeat. I run from the bank and charge into the forest, coming back with a huge branch that's ten times longer than me.

"Listen!" I shout. "I'm going to hold this out to you – you need to grab it with your teeth, OK?"

Jaxon's eyes widen. "I'll fall."

"You have to!"

It's now or never. I pick up the branch in my mouth and lean it across the gap between us. It still doesn't quite reach him. If Jaxon wants to grab the stick, he's going to have to jump.

The log Jaxon's clinging to is slipping – I can see it's going to break. I watch Jaxon make the choice. He gives one final great heave, throws himself from the log, twists his head around…

And grabs the branch with his teeth. He lands in the

water, almost wrenching me in with him, but I dig my paws into the bank and clamp down. It's agony – my jaw turns to concrete with the strain of holding him – but it's working. I step backwards, inch by inch, and Jaxon paddles furiously to the shore until the water's shallow enough for him to clamber onto the bank. He hardly has the strength for that – he collapses to the ground, panting for breath. He's alive! Shaken and trembling, but alive.

"Jaxon!" I ask, running over to him. "Are you all right?"

"No," he gasps. "I'm not."

He glares up at me, soaking wet and furious.

"You've just saved my life *again*," he says. "Which means if I ever want to be free from you, I have to save your life *twice*."

21
CAVE

I beam from ear to ear. Jaxon is complaining. That means he's OK!

But then he tries to stand, and I see he *isn't* OK. The moment he puts his back paw on the ground, he yelps with pain and falls down again.

"Jaxon?" I ask.

"I'm fine," he insists.

But he's lying. He tries again, and it's even worse the second time. He can't walk – he's hurt. And that's bad, bad news. How can Jaxon climb a mountain with an injured paw?

He shifts on the ground. "You go on ahead," he says. He's trying to sound light, but his voice comes out fake and thin. "I'll rest here until I'm better, then catch up with you."

He's right. I have to keep going – if I don't, I could miss my chance to find Tom.

But there's no way I can keep going without Jaxon. I *need* him. I don't know the way to the High Castle. Besides, I can't leave him here, alone and injured … can I?

I glance around. We're in the middle of the wilderness. Night is going to fall soon, and when it does, it's going to get cold. *Really* cold. There might even be wolves. We need to find shelter *now*. "Get up. We have to find somewhere for you to rest."

"You have to go, Rebel," says Jaxon, his voice hardening. "If you don't get moving—"

"No!" I bark. "I'm not leaving you!"

Jaxon glares at me, but there's fear in his eyes too. "I can't walk, Rebel." His voice is very small.

I grit my teeth. "You have to do what I say, remember? So come on! Get up!"

I feel terrible for making Jaxon move when he's clearly in so much pain, but we don't have a choice. He gets to his feet shakily, lifting his bad paw in the air so he doesn't have to step on it.

"Good," I say. "Now lean against me, as much as you can."

"I can't lean against you; you're tiny!"

"Stop arguing and do it!"

We slowly, *slowly* limp our way over the stony ground. Neither of us talks. At first, I think Jaxon isn't speaking because he's mad at me – but then I realize it's because he's using every scrap of his energy to stop himself howling with pain.

My stomach is a knot. What on earth are we going to do? We're supposed to be climbing this mountain right now, racing to find Tom before it's too late. But Jaxon desperately needs somewhere safe to rest. I scan the mountainside for a broken log that might provide us with shelter, but there's *nothing*. There's a few trees and bushes around us, and the rest of the mountain is solid rock.

Then I see something up ahead. A cave, tucked into the mountain wall.

"Over here!"

I lead Jaxon hobbling to the cave entrance. It's cool and dark inside, with an opening just big enough for us to crawl through. Small is good: it'll keep in more heat, and protect us better too. I let Jaxon slump against the back wall and sink down on his haunches, struggling for breath.

I look at him, curled into a corner, and realize how much trouble we're in. Jaxon is silent and scared, his ears pressed flat to his head. He looks like a dying animal. I realize, for the first time, how old he is. His fur is grey and fading. He's not going to get over an injury like this easily. He might *never* get over it. What's the rest of his life going to be like, if he can't feed himself or even get water?

Jaxon stares at me.

"Rebel," he whispers. "Listen to me. You need to go on alone, while you still can."

My fur stands on end. "No."

"Yes," he says. "I don't know how long it'll take me to get better. If you stay here, you won't find Tom in time. Is that what you want?"

The thought is too horrible to bear thinking about. Jaxon's right again. If I don't leave now, I could lose my chance to save Tom. He could get swallowed up by the storm cloud of war. He could *die*.

But if I leave Jaxon here, he could die too. Alone, in a cave, in pain. I can't do that.

"I'm not going anywhere."

"But—" Jaxon tries.

"No!" I bark. "You're supposed to do what I say. So, so … stay here and get better while I find us some food!"

I run out of the cave before he can argue with me. I've made my choice – I'm staying here. I won't leave Jaxon behind, no matter how much I need to find Tom. I *can't*. Maybe if I find us some food, Jaxon will get better faster, and then we can leave and everything will be fine.

But how am I going to find food? I've never hunted before. The closest I've come is the accidental sheep bite, and there aren't going to be sheep out here in the wilderness. There'll be birds and rabbits, but they've spent their whole lives learning how to not get eaten. I start to panic. What am I going to do if I can't hunt? Are Jaxon and I *both* going to die here, trapped between the river and the…

I stop. Then I blink a few times, because I can't believe what I'm seeing.

It's a lamb, standing amongst the trees before me. It's alone. It's stumbling around in circles, looking confused.

"Lost," it bleats. "Looooooost."

My heart pounds. It's a miracle! Even *I* can hunt a little lamb. Jaxon and I can eat! We're saved!

But am I *really* going to kill a lamb? It's just a baby, looking for its mother. Good dogs don't kill lambs. I'm not a bad dog, am I?

But if I don't hunt the lamb, Jaxon won't get better. And if Jaxon doesn't get better, then I'll never get to the High Castle. If I don't get to the High Castle, then I can't save Tom.

I creep forward and crouch behind a fern, keeping the lamb fixed in my sights. It still hasn't seen me. One good leap, one bite, and it'll all be over.

"Lost," bleats the lamb. "Loooost."

I swallow. I don't want to do this. But I *have* to do this. For me. For Jaxon. For Tom.

I crouch down low, ready to jump…

Click.

It takes me a second to recognize the sound behind me. It's the sound of a gun being cocked.

"Sorry, pal," says a steady voice. "Not today."

I turn around, and find myself gazing straight down the barrel of a loaded rifle.

22

POL

 I stare at the rifle, and my whole life flashes before my eyes.

Tom.

Lamb stew.

Mum and Dad.

Top Field.

Tom.

Barking at Priscilla when she's asleep and making her fall in the pond.

Lamb stew.

That time I found a bit of chicken on the floor.

Rolling in fox poo and jumping on Mum and Dad's bed.

The bone I buried in Bottom Field – I've forgotten about that!

Lamb stew.

Tom.

The rifle halts in mid-air; the barrel lowers. It's a young girl, even younger than Tom. She has a sheepskin cape tied loosely around her with a woven cord and is wearing a leather cap on her head.

"Oh! Sorry," she says. "Thought you were a wild dog."

She shoulders the rifle and strolls over to the lamb, picking it up in one hand.

"Honestly, it's like these things don't even *want* to live sometimes," she sighs. "Why come down here if you don't know how to get back up, eh?"

"Loooost," bleats the lamb.

She shoves the lamb into a pouch slung over her side. The lamb pokes its head out, bleats once more, and then immediately falls asleep. The girl walks over and kneels down to look at me. I let her do it, partly because she seems nice, but also because I'm still frozen stiff with terror and can't move. She smells of wool, and woodsmoke, and the forest after it rains.

"Hmm. I don't know *what* you are, but you're *definitely* not a wild dog. What's a scraggy old mutt like you doing out here in the wilderness, eh?"

Rude. I'm about to bark at her for saying I'm scraggy, but then she reaches out a hand and scratches my head … and I melt. It's been so, so long since someone scratched my head. I've forgotten how much I've missed it. All this running, all these hungry days and cold nights, all this time without Tom … it's taken its toll on me. It's left me hard and hollow inside. The moment the girl rubs my head, all that disappears. I close my eyes blissfully. It's like I'm home again.

"I'm Pol," says the girl. "What are you doing down here by the caves, mystery dog?"

My eyes snap open. *Jaxon!* I jump up and bark. "Quick! You have to come with me!"

Pol holds up her hands, surprised. "Hey. Don't worry. I'm not going to hurt you."

She doesn't understand me. I *have* to make her understand. I spin around in circles and wag my tail to show I'm not angry, then run a few steps towards the cave and turn around and bark again.

"This way, please!"

Pol frowns. "You want me to follow you?"

"Yes! Over here!"

I run a couple of feet at a time, stopping every few seconds and barking to make sure Pol's still following. When I finally enter the cave, Jaxon is pressed against the back wall, wet and shaking. He looks even worse than when I left him.

"What's going on?" he asks quietly. "I thought I heard barking…"

Pol crouches down at the cave entrance and peers inside. "Hey! There's two of you!"

Jaxon's eyes turn white with terror. He rears back, snarling and baring his teeth. *"Go away! Get back!"*

Pol staggers in surprise. It's horrible: Jaxon's trembling, his eyes full of hate. He glares at me. "Why did you bring her here?"

"I think she can help," I say. "She's a shepherd and—"

"You stupid house dog – look at her!" Jaxon roars. "She's got a gun! She could kill us! Don't you understand that not every human is—"

He falters on his bad paw and howls with agony, almost collapsing again. Pol spots it straight away. "Your paw. You're hurt."

"Jaxon," I say steadily. "You need to let her look at your paw."

Jaxon grits his teeth. "If she touches me, I'll bite her hand off."

"No, you won't!" I snap. "Because I've saved your life *twice*! And if you don't do what I say, so help me, *I'm* going to kill you!"

It's the loudest I've ever shouted at anyone, ever. Jaxon doesn't reply. We just glare at each other in silence. Pol glances between us.

"OK – that was weird," she mutters.

Pol carefully removes the rifle from her shoulder and places it on the ground outside. Then she slowly shuffles into the cave, her hands low and open beside her, showing Jaxon that she's safe, checking with every step to see how he's responding. Jaxon stays where he is, not moving.

"That's it," says Pol, keeping her voice calm and gentle. "I'm not going to hurt you. I'm just saying hello."

I believe every word that she says; I know she isn't

going to hurt Jaxon. She slowly lifts the back of her hand and holds it out so he can smell her.

"See? I'm safe." She inches forward again. "I'm going to take a look at your paw. I'm not going to touch it; I just want to make sure it isn't broken."

"Rebel…" says Jaxon nervously.

"Let her do it," I say.

Pol reaches out, slow and steady, and moves aside his tail, which is curled up tight against his bad paw. Jaxon flinches and keeps his head turned away, but he doesn't try to stop her. He's shaking from head to foot. He looks absolutely terrified.

"OK – I don't think it's broken." Pol sighs. "I think you just need some proper rest and a few good meals. You both do; you look exhausted."

She's right. We *are* exhausted.

"I can't do much to help you down here," says Pol. "But I can take you to Grandad. We live further up the mountain together. He'll be able to check your paw properly – he'll know how to make it better too. I can take you there, if you'll let me." She glances at Jaxon. "It means I'll have to carry you."

"No!" he barks. "I am *not* going to let her carry me!"

"Yes, you are," I say. "If you stay down here, you'll die."

"No, I won't," says Jaxon quickly. "I just need to rest for a bit and—"

"Jaxon." I shake my head. "I'm not letting you stay here."

He gives me a look that's so furious I think he might bite me. But he doesn't. Instead he lowers his head, limps from the wall, and presents himself to Pol.

She smiles warmly. "Oh! That was easy. OK, I'm going to pick you up now…"

She reaches her arms under Jaxon's chest and heaves him gently off the ground, then she staggers back until she's out of the cave again.

"*Ugh*, you stink," Pol mutters. "I think both of you could do with a bath too."

Jaxon glares at me with horror. *"Rebel…"*

"All right, all right, you don't have to have a bath," I say.

Pol shifts Jaxon so that he's slung across her shoulders, moving as carefully as she can so she doesn't touch his paw, then starts striding up the mountain. I follow close at her heels. It's slower going than before, because Pol's carrying Jaxon and the lamb, but she does a good job. She's stronger than she looks.

She finds a well-worn path that twists up the rock face, and slowly, step by step, we climb the mountain. It's hard work; we have to squeeze through nooks and crannies and scramble up steep slopes. I'm quickly out of breath, but Pol never breaks stride. She's clearly done this thousands of times before. Inch by inch, the treetops slip away, until they look little more than shrubs beneath us.

Then at last Pol heaves herself up one final slope and stands on flat ground.

"There!" she pants. "All done. The chimney's on – Grandad must be home."

I can hear that she's talking, but I'm not really listening. I'm too busy staring at what lies ahead of me, speechless. We're halfway up the mountain. In front of us, sheltered on three sides by rock walls, is a flat plain rich with grass and wild flowers. Dozens of the biggest, fattest, happiest sheep I've ever seen are grazing peacefully in front of us. In the middle of it, tucked like an egg in a nest, is a little wooden hut. The roof and sides are covered in turf, so it almost looks like part of the mountain itself. And just as Pol said, smoke is curling from the chimney.

"Come on!" she says, striding ahead. "Let's go find Grandad."

23

GRANDAD

*P*ol makes her way towards the hut with Jaxon balanced across her shoulders. The lamb has jumped out of the pouch and is stumbling through the grass, bleating in confusion and looking for its mother. I follow Pol, nudging the lamb in the right direction. I might not be able to hunt, but I can do *this* like the back of my paw.

"That's it!" I say. "This way, please. No, don't eat that. Come on!"

Up ahead, a man has stepped from the hut and is watching us approach. He's wearing identical clothes to the girl, but his skin is so old and weathered it's hard to tell where the leather cap ends and his face begins. He barely even blinks as his granddaughter approaches with two stray dogs.

"I found them down by the caves," she says.

Grandad crouches down and pats my head. He smells of hot embers from the fire. When he speaks, his voice is rough and warm, like a wooden flute. "Well, well. Aren't we a top-notch little fella?"

I wag my tail. I *am* a top-notch little fella.

Pol half turns to show him Jaxon on her shoulders. "This one's hurt his back paw. Can you take a look?"

Grandad sighs and nods. "If he'll let me. Go get the sheep in for the night and I'll see what I can do."

Pol hands Jaxon over, and skips off to the flock without another word. Grandad carries Jaxon into the hut and I scuttle after them before the door slams shut on my tail.

The hut is close and dim and warm inside. There's a fresh fire crackling in the centre, with a stone pot bubbling on top. The smell stops me in my tracks; my heart sings and my mouth begins to water. It's—

"Yep – lamb stew," says Grandad, nodding at me. "Try and take any, dog, and I'll throw you right in the pot with it. But if you're good, there might be a bone or two I can give you later."

Lamb bones. I think I'm going to die of happiness.

Grandad lowers Jaxon onto a heap of sacking near the fire and studies him carefully.

"Right," he says at last. "I'm going to look at that paw. I know you don't want me to, but I need to see what we're dealing with."

Jaxon looks so small and frightened. "Rebel," he whispers. "What if he hurts me?"

"It's going to be all right," I say. "I promise."

Grandad reaches out and carefully, oh so carefully, takes Jaxon's paw in his hand. Jaxon immediately yelps and snatches it away, but Grandad shushes him.

"It's OK! It's OK. The good news is, it's definitely not broken. You just need something for the swelling. I've got a poultice here that'll help."

He stands up and starts rummaging through some stone jars at the back of the hut. He talks as he does, filling the hut with his gentle babble just like Pol did in the cave, to let us know that he's not a threat.

"Not often we get visitors up here. We see plenty of birds and rabbits, maybe a few deer sometimes, but never dogs. Most of the time it's just me and Pol.

And the sheep, of course." He comes back with a jar of ointment. "I always give them this when they sprain their hooves. It'll hurt when I first put it on, but you'll feel much better for it, I promise."

Jaxon glances at me, and back at Grandad, and braces himself. Grandad takes a big handful of the ointment, fresh as wet stone and bitter with herbs, and carefully dabs it on Jaxon's paw. Jaxon doesn't even wince.

"Good boy," says Grandad gently. "Right – it's time you both got washed; you absolutely stink. Lucky for you I just heated this up."

He heaves over a copper kettle the size of a pumpkin and empties it into a metal tub on the floor, humming under his breath. "Right! You can go first, big dog…"

"*No!*" Jaxon roars.

Grandad backs off immediately. "All right! No bath for you." He turns to me. "Anyone else for a…?"

"*ME!*" I shout.

I fling myself headfirst into the water, and feel the rich warmth immediately rush into my bones. I am in heaven. After so many cold days and nights, it's like drinking in a month of summers. I spin and froth in circles, rolling over and wagging my tail so hard it sends water spraying in every direction. By the time I'm done, Grandad is completely soaked and laughing so hard he's started coughing. Jaxon is staring at me with disgust.

"Look at you," he mutters. "You've spent *days* trying to dry off. One nod from a human and you're back in the water."

"There is a *big* difference," I say, "between water you choose, and water you don't choose."

I climb out of the tub and lie beside the fire to steam myself dry. Grandad settles down to fuss over the stew, steadily chopping vegetables into the pot as it tocks and bubbles. After a while, Pol comes back and announces that the sheep are safely stowed inside their cave for the night. The room fills with the warm familiar patter of human chat and the rich smell of lamb stew until the whole hut is hugged with it. When the stew is finally done, Grandad spoons out a bowl for himself and another for Pol.

"Grandad," murmurs Pol.

He glances at me and Jaxon, both staring at him and drooling rivers.

He chuckles. "Huh. Where are my manners?!"

He plucks a couple of objects out of the pot and chucks them on the floor – one for me, and another for Jaxon. My nose lights up like a bonfire. Lamb bones, heavy with wobbling hunks of fat and dripping in gravy. Hunting is all well and good, but this is *hot* food, and there is *nothing* on earth like hot food. I dive on my bone like a dog possessed, licking and chomping and gnawing like I haven't eaten in ten years. Jaxon does the same, keeping one beady eye fixed on the others the whole time.

"They like it!" Pol laughs delightedly. "Can we keep them, Grandad?"

Grandad shakes his head. "No, Pol. They can stay if they like, but…"

"I know," she groans. "Not everything's a pet."

Grandad leans over and picks at my neckerchief. "Looks like this one was travelling with the Reds. They must have been using the old sheep trails to get around and got lost. That'd make sense. No chance of being stopped by the King's guardsmen on those trails. They're the one place left which that bloodthirsty tyrant doesn't control."

Pol swallows a scalding mouthful of stew. "Didn't you ever want to join the Reds?"

Grandad looks sad for a moment, gloom passing across his eyes like clouds. "My brother did, back when the King first took the throne. Then one day some guardsmen came looking for him, and he had to run away. I haven't seen him since." He sighs. "I moved us out here not long after. Home just didn't feel the same any more."

"You never thought about looking for him?" Pol asks.

"Course I did," says Grandad. "But I had you to look after, didn't I? Best thing that ever happened to me." He ruffles her hair. "I do miss him, though. I'd give anything to see him again. Still – that's the price you pay for being lucky enough to have more than one person to love, isn't it?"

They finish eating, and the rest of the evening passes by in cosy silence. I sit and drink it all in, watching Grandad's pipe smoke drift to the top of the thatch and Pol's steady hand as she carves a piece of wood. We listen as the clouds drift over the valley, speckling rain against the turf, breathing wind beneath the door to make the fire swell.

It's like I never left the farm. I wonder if Tom is thinking about it. I wonder if he's thinking about me. I hope he's safe and warm and happy, wherever he is.

"Not bad, eh?" I murmur to Jaxon.

He glances at Pol and Grandad warily. "Hmm. For now. But we still should be careful."

I shake my head. "I don't understand you. You make out like all humans are evil and everything is bad. Good things happen too, you know."

"Such as?" he asks sarcastically.

I think about it. "Well – *you*, for a start. If you hadn't found me on the trail, I'd have died. That was a good thing. Finding Pol and Grandad was a good thing too. They're helping us."

"Accepting help from humans always has a price," says Jaxon drily.

I frown. "What about me and Tom? There's no price to that. We just love each other."

Jaxon laughs. "Love *is* a price, Rebel. To be loved by humans, you *have* to belong to them. Don't you see that?" He nods to the fire. "That's the trade we animals always have to make. We give up our freedom, our power, our self-respect, in return for a bit of warmth and scraps from their table." He settles down to sleep. "Forget that. I'd rather die free than spend the rest of my days here, living like a prisoner for food."

I bristle. Part of me still wants to tell Jaxon that he's wrong. Part of me wants to tell him that being with someone you love and who loves you is the best thing in the world...

But the problem is, I don't think he *is* wrong. Not completely, anyway. I've never felt freer, never more like myself, than I have running through the mountains over the last few days. Jaxon called it "finding my True Dog" – does that mean I won't truly be myself, when I'm back on the farm with Tom? He would always want me to go where he goes, to come when he calls, to stay where he tells me. I could never have that kind of freedom again.

But maybe some things are worth giving up. No, not *giving up*...

Oh, I don't know what the word is. Even thinking about it makes my head hurt. Jaxon always seems to know immediately when things are right and things are wrong, but I don't know if all answers are that simple. All I know is there's something beautiful about us all sitting together in this hut, sharing our warmth, dogs and humans seeing out the night together. And no matter what Jaxon says, I can't help but notice that he closes his eyes with pleasure when Grandad reaches over and scratches the fur behind his ears.

A
DARK
DAY

24
FOREST

I'm anxious to move on as soon as we can, but there's no point until Jaxon's paw has properly healed. And frankly, there are worse places to wait. I spend the next day outside with Pol while Jaxon recovers at the hut with Grandad. At first, Jaxon hates it, but he relaxes soon enough. I think he's grateful to have some rest. In fact, he seems more at home than I've ever seen him before.

The view from up here on the mountain is unbelievable. I stand among the wildflowers and gaze out across the world while the wind ruffles its fingers through my fur. I can see so much more than I ever could from Top Field: miles of rolling grass, stretches of cloud, the sunlight as it dips past the horizon. I even spot a neighbouring mountain that's carpeted in daisies from top to bottom, like a waterfall.

Daisies all the way down. If only Tom could see this.

And that makes me worried. The world is so peaceful up here, but Tom is somewhere down there, marching towards the High Castle. The battle might even have started by now. Tom is still in danger. We're running out of time.

Luckily, the poultice on Jaxon's paw works wonders. By the next morning, he can put weight on it, and by the morning after *that* he can walk on it without limping. We've waited long enough – it's time for us to go.

The moment we step out of the hut on the third day, Pol seems to twig what's going on.

"Oh – you're leaving?"

My tail wags sadly. I want to thank Pol for all her help, for saving Jaxon and for looking after us ... but I can't do any of that, because I'm a dog. So I just lick her hand instead. That seems to do the trick.

"Well, it was nice meeting you," says Pol. "Maybe we'll see one another again some day."

She rubs my head softly, and then Jaxon's, before striding out to the sheep without a backward glance.

"See?" I say to Jaxon. "I told you they were nice."

Jaxon snorts. "Sure."

I shuffle uneasily. I've been thinking about this a lot over the last two days. "This would be a good place to stay, you know. When all this is done."

Jaxon glances at me. "What do you mean?"

"Well – when I've found Tom and head back home, and your debt is repaid," I say. The words tumble out in a rush. "You can't be alone for the rest of your life, can you? It's nice up here. Pol and Grandad would take care of you." I pause before I say the next bit. "You know … when you get old."

Jaxon turns away from me. The silence between us turns to stone.

"Come on," he says eventually. "The gorge is this way."

And with that, he marches up the slope. I decide it's best not to push it. Besides, this is it: our final stretch. The High Castle is somewhere on the other side of this mountain. After two days of rest and some decent food, I feel more ready to find Tom than ever. I only hope we're not already too late.

We climb all morning, until the ground finally flattens out. We pause for a moment, and gaze down the steep incline below us. This side of the mountain is thick with forest, but I can tell as soon as we enter that there's something wrong with it. The trees are tall and wide, their canopies spread like vultures' wings above us, so no sunlight can reach the forest floor. It smells dead, and dry, and *sick*. Nothing grows here; there's no visible path, either. We keep getting lost, turning back on ourselves whenever the forest ends in a sheer rocky cliff.

The landscape isn't the only thing that feels wrong. Jaxon isn't speaking to me – he's barely looking at me. I can feel the bad mood burning off him, and it's getting worse and worse the more lost we become. Finally he stops dead, roaring with frustration.

"Great! I can't find the path that I used before," he snarls. "We'll have to go all the way back to Unsk and start over. I told you we should *never* have followed that girl!"

I can't help but bristle at that. "Pol saved your life, Jaxon."

"So? I never asked her to!" he snaps back. "I went with her because you *made* me, Rebel. Everything was *fine* until I met you!"

I'm shocked. Jaxon is angry in a way that I haven't seen before. He paces the forest floor like a trapped animal.

"Before I met you, I was Masterless," he growls. "I did what I wanted, when I wanted. Now I'm stuck with you, and there's nothing I can do about it!"

I grit my teeth. I'm starting to feel angry too. "You know what? Being alone isn't so great, Jaxon. The Companion isn't going to feed you when you're sick, or look after you when you're old. You need more than that!"

Jaxon sneers at me. "That's why you're dragging yourself halfway across the country, is it? For a few bones and a pat on the head?"

I feel my blood boil. "I didn't see you complaining when Grandad was patting your head the other night!"

The look Jaxon gives me is hot with shame: shame at allowing himself to be petted; shame at seeming weak for even a moment. A bad feeling is settling between us. Thick grey mist has drifted down from the mountain top, making everything seem blurred and wrong.

"Listen to yourself," Jaxon spits. "You're so home-fed, you don't even know what makes you *real* any more. Wearing that stupid neckerchief, all because some *boy* gave it to you—"

"It's not stupid!" I bark.

"It is, and so are you!" he snaps. "You're too stupid to question anything in your life. Too stupid to see that you deserve more than whatever a human decides to hand to you. Too stupid to see that Tom doesn't feel the same way about you that you feel about him!"

It's like being struck. Jaxon is saying the worst things possible, the things I've feared more than anything, things I couldn't even admit to myself. But he keeps going.

"Would Tom do all this for you? Run across the country, almost get himself killed ten times over? If you called for him, would he come running for *you*? Because I can't help but feel that if he *did* love you, Rebel, then he never would have left you in the first place." He shakes his head in pity. "Don't you see? Tom doesn't *need* you any more. You have to forget about him, like he's forgotten about you."

His words freeze me to the spot. The words I want to say back to him burn my mouth like salt. But once again, the worst part about what Jaxon says – the part that hurts the most – is that he's not wrong. There's a reason why I'm not in Tom's drawings any more. A reason why he hasn't come home. A reason why he left me behind.

Tom doesn't need me any more. He's moved on. He's grown up, and found new things to love.

But I can't stop loving him.

And that's the truth of it. It doesn't *matter* if Tom has forgotten about me. If you love someone, and that person is in danger, then you have to save them. Jaxon could never understand that. And if I have to find Tom on my own, then so be it.

"You still have to do what I tell you, right?" I say, my voice shaking. "So leave. Go and find somewhere else to be. Somewhere you'll be happy. But you know what, Jaxon? I don't think you'll ever find it."

Jaxon flinches. The forest seems colder all of a sudden; the wind moans, clashing the trees against one another.

We stand apart. I can feel something awful filling the space between us. It's … *nothing*. After everything we've been through, after everything we've faced together, the friendship that we forged together is as dead as this forest.

"Suit yourself," says Jaxon quietly. "Goodbye, Reb—"

A sound cuts through the forest – a terrible sound, a sound that travels up from my paws and rattles in my chest, low and somehow high at the same time – and the moment I hear it, I know exactly what's making it. And I know how close they are.

It's the howl of a wolf. And it's followed by another, and another, and another.

The pack has surrounded us. There are dozens of them, gathering between the trees and closing around us like a snare. They must have been following us for miles, slinking into place while we were arguing, blocking off every escape until there's nowhere left for us to run.

We're trapped.

25

WOLF

The wolves step closer towards us in the fog. Their fur is thick and ragged; their snouts are long and sharp; their shoulders are boned and bristling. Every movement nicks the air around them like blades. I always imagined that wolves would smell like fire, but they don't. They smell like spit. Spit and blood.

The biggest one steps forward. I know right away that it's the leader: he's huge, even bigger than Jaxon. The length of his snout is knotted with scars, some fresh, some old.

"Well," he growls, his voice rippling at the edges, "it's not often we find dogs out here in the wilderness."

I've never been so frightened. I can barely even

stand, I'm trembling so hard. But Jaxon stays strong, his head level and his gaze steady.

"We're not seeking any fight," he says calmly, addressing the leader. "We're just passing through."

The wolves howl with laughter. The noise locks me to the ground with terror.

"Fight?" says the leader incredulously. "If there *was* a fight, dog, there wouldn't be much you could do about it."

He paces through the trees towards us, taking a slow and twisting route. He doesn't need to rush: he knows there's nowhere we can run. Jaxon stays facing the wolf leader, not even blinking. He doesn't look old any more; he doesn't look wounded. He looks strong. It's like there's dozens of him and only one wolf, instead of the other way around.

"Forgive us," he says quietly. "We didn't know this was your territory. We're leaving now."

"Leave?" the leader replies. "No, dog, we cannot let you do that. Once, we might have done, but not now."

The leader continues his slow approach towards us, until he's barely a stone's throw away.

"The last few years have not been kind to wolves," he says. "There was a time when humans would bring their sheep into the mountains. Enough to keep us in blood. But that time is long past. Ever since the coming of the human King, the shepherds have stayed away from the wilderness. The King sends his own hunters up here instead, taking every animal for himself. Now the mountains are dead, and my wolves are starving."

The wolves are steadily closing in around us, their shapes becoming clearer in the fog. I can see the lean outline of their bodies, the bulging ribs beneath their ragged fur, the hunger gleaming in the cold stars of their eyes. I stumble back to Jaxon and cower between his legs.

"Jaxon … we're going to die," I whimper.

"No, we're not," Jaxon whispers, his voice as steady as his gaze. "We're going to run."

I stare at him in horror. *Run?* How can we run? There's no way out. The wolves have us trapped. Jaxon's leg has only just healed. But I watch him close his eyes and take a deep breath.

"Wherever I go," he whispers to himself, "the Companion walks with me."

The leader stops in front of us. His whole body tenses, like the first lightning flash before the thunder breaks, then he rockets forward, launching himself through the air.

Jaxon leaps to meet him, knocking him back and pinning him to the ground. The other wolves tear through the trees, all white eyes and foaming teeth, but Jaxon scrambles up and dodges them at the last second, turning to me.

"Behind you!" he shouts.

I swing around just in time – a wolf is flying out of the fog, blood-hungry jaws wide open. Jaxon soars over my head, sending it tumbling down the hill.

"Run, Rebel!" he cries.

I don't know what to do. I can't leave Jaxon to fight these wolves alone ... but if I stay, I'll die. I tear down the slope as fast as I can, half falling and half weaving between the trees, terror pulsing through my mouth and blood pounding in my veins. My paws barely brush the ground as I fly through the forest – one wrong step, one trip, and I'm done for. I have to get off this mountain!

But I can hear paws hammering the hard earth behind me, and I know they aren't Jaxon's. I steal a terrified glance over my shoulder and there's the lead wolf, crashing like an avalanche towards me. I can hear the heave of his breath and the scrape of his claws on the forest floor as he gets closer and closer…

And then the trees end, and my stomach drops.

There's no ground left. Up ahead is a lone dagger outcrop of rock, and then nothing but miles of thin air. I scramble to the edge, praying that there's some hidden path I can climb down, but there's nothing. Just a sheer drop, plummeting hundreds of feet to another forest floor.

"That's far enough for you, little dog," says a mocking voice behind me.

I turn around, petrified. The lead wolf is stepping out of the trees, a hungry smile peeling down the length of his snout.

"L-leave me alone!" I bark, shaking with terror.

The leader doesn't listen. He takes another step towards me, his movements soft and deliberate. There's nowhere left for me to go. There's a sheer drop behind me and a wall of teeth ahead. My eyes are blurring with panic. It's over. I'm going to die.

It must be the fear that does it. Suddenly everything seems very simple, very clear. It's me against the wolf. I *have* to fight. I have to find the strength to survive.

So I dig deep, and I find the one true thing that gives me strength.

Tom.

I think about us lying under the blankets, breathing together.

I think about sitting by his side as we watch the sunset together.

I think about how it feels to run to him when he calls.

I think about all the different monsters that I would fight, all the mountains that I would climb, just to be with him for one more second.

And that's when I find it: my True Dog. The part of me that's alive, the part of me that's wild, the part of me that knows what it means to breathe air and run and feel every heartbeat. The part of me that's come all this way for love. I feel it burst in my chest like a sunrise and course through me like fire. And this time, when I stand against the wolf, I don't feel small at all. I feel as wide as the sky. I feel as strong as the mountain.

I am Rebel, and I'm not frightened any more.

"Let me go," I growl.

The wolf laughs. "There's some fight in you, little dog. I'm going to enjoy this."

I leap forward and snap at him, catching the skin of his snout. The wolf flinches backwards in shock.

"Let. Me. Go!" I growl again.

Furious, the wolf snarls and flings himself at me. I throw myself to the ground, and the wolf's jaws barely miss my ear as he sails over me. The wolf slams his paws on the bare rock as he awkwardly spins around to make the killing blow, but he can't stop himself. He's being carried backwards by his own weight, his claws scrabbling on the stone. He makes one final desperate lunge for me as he skids over the mountain's edge, his flailing limbs catching me and dragging me towards him, sending me rolling with the force of the blow and tumbling over the side of the cliff...

And then I'm plummeting in a scattering of loose

rock and howling wind, pinwheeling towards the trees as the forest rises up with a speed that seems impossible, everything looming bigger and faster and closer as the great dark canopy swallows me whole…

26

PATH

I open my eyes.

I'm lying on the ground. That's weird. The last thing I remember was falling off a cliff.

I should be dead. Instead, I've somehow fallen through the trees and landed on a forest path – but there are no signs of any broken branches around me.

Then I remember – the wolf. If *I'm* alive, then he's probably alive too! I leap to my feet…

And pause. There's no wolf. But there *is* another dog, sitting on the path beside me.

"Hello," says the dog.

The dog doesn't look like any other dog I've ever seen. Their fur is soft and grey; their eyes are grey too. But for some reason, I feel like I've always known them.

I can't smell them, though. Maybe the fall damaged my nose.

"That was quite a tumble," says the strange dog. "How do you feel?"

I think about it. I don't seem to have a single injury. In fact, I don't have *any* aches and pains. "Great, actually," I say at last. I glance around. "You haven't seen a wolf, have you?"

The strange dog shakes their head. "Don't think so."

It must have landed somewhere else. I look at the mountain above. Jaxon's still up there; he could be looking for me – or fighting for his life. "Is there another way back up?" I ask.

"Maybe," says the strange dog. "Why don't we walk for a while, and see what we find?"

The dog starts to walk away. I scamper to catch up, and we stroll side by side along the path. I should be worried about Jaxon, or the wolf leader – but for some reason, I don't feel worried at all. The forest is beautiful, much nicer than the wilderness above us. Great slants of sunlight cut through the trees, lighting up the waves of bugs and pollen. I've never seen so many beautiful flowers. They're every single colour that you can think of, and they cover every inch of the forest floor. Maybe this is what a carpet looks like, I think. No wonder people like them.

Suddenly I freeze. I've just seen an animal in the trees ahead of us. Is it Jaxon? Or the wolf? I peer through the trees to get a better look...

It's another dog. But it's not Jaxon; it's a mother, lying in a pool of golden flowers with a litter of puppies. I can't believe it – what on earth are they doing out here, when there are wolves about? I leave the path and race to warn her—

And stop. I recognize the dog, licking her children as they feed from her. I would know her *anywhere*. Her smell, her fur...

"That's my mother," I say.

I always wondered what happened to her. I always wondered what she looked like. But the strange dog doesn't react. They just keep walking. "Come on. This way."

Part of me doesn't want to go. Part of me wants to stay here with my mother, and never leave her again.

But I've just spotted something else in the forest, further along the path. A person, kneeling down… I recognize them too. My heart leaps.

"Tom!"

He's here! I've found him! I charge through the flowers to reach him, barking with happiness…

And stop again. The flowers have vanished; the ground around me is blanketed in snow. I'm standing in the middle of a winter night.

The Tom that kneels before me isn't the Tom I last saw at the farm. He's young, maybe six or seven years old. He's leaning down to scoop something out of the snow and bundle it into his coat.

It's a puppy. And not just any puppy – it's me. It's the moment that Tom found me alone and dying in the cold, and took me home.

I'm watching the moment he saved me.

"Where am I?" I ask, turning to the strange dog. "What is this place?"

The dog looks kindly at me, their eyes as calm and grey as deep waters. "Come. There's more for you to see."

So I keep walking. And wherever I look, I see

something new. There's me and Tom, running through Top Field together. There's me, hiding under his chair, and Tom feeding me bits of his breakfast. There he is, sitting with Mum and Dad by the fire while I spread across their laps, held in their happy warmth.

"These are all me," I marvel. "These are all different parts of my life."

"I know, Rebel," says the dog. "I was with you."

I turn to ask how they know my name, but the dog isn't walking any more. They're sitting at the edge of the forest. The path has ended, and I can see what lies beyond.

It's a cornfield. I've never seen anywhere so beautiful before. It shifts and sways like waves of gold in the sun, and the smell is all summer, fresh and pure and full of promise. The field goes on for miles, on until for ever, to a place where the sun is always shining and there are no mountains or wilderness to get in the way. Like a carpet, I think.

No – not like a carpet. Like a sea. Maybe *this* is what the sea looks like.

Something is racing away from us, bounding with

joy and parting the corn as they go. It's the wolf leader. He's running as fast as he can, barking and barking and barking like a puppy.

"You can go too, if you like," says the strange dog.

I want to go – but I'm afraid. "Won't the wolf hurt me?"

The strange dog shakes their head. "Nothing hurts where he's going."

I believe it. I can feel the cornfield calling me, making my whole body sing like an unbroken note. I know that when I run into the field, everything will be beautiful, for ever and ever. Everything will be perfect.

Only it can't be perfect.

I gaze back at the path we've just taken. I see Tom, and Tom, and Tom, over and over again. There he is, twelve and tall for his age, sketching in the last of the day's sun. There he is wandering downstairs in the morning, rubbing sleep from his eyes. There he is, feeding me tenderly by hand, calling me Little Belly.

Tom's not in the cornfield. He's back *there*. And if I leave now, he can't go with me. Not yet anyway. Not for a long time.

And that's not all I see in the trees. I can see me and Jaxon too, running side by side.

I gaze back beyond the forest, above the trees. The mountain that I left seems so much darker now, so much colder, so much more real and painful. But Jaxon is up there. I can't leave him behind.

"I'm sorry," I say to the dog. "You've been very kind to me. But I can't go just yet. I have friends who need me."

The strange dog gives me a final smile.

"I had a feeling you'd say that," says the Companion. "So long, Rebel. We'll meet again one day."

27

BRANCH

"*Rebel!*"

Everything is dark.

The world is spinning. I hurt all over.

"*Rebel!*"

Someone is calling me.

"*Can you hear me? Rebel!*"

The voice is coming from below. I open my eyes. I'm not lying on the ground: I'm hanging in mid-air. Jaxon is on the forest floor beneath me, calling up to me. There's something lying still beside him. It's the wolf leader, surrounded by broken branches. He's dead.

"Rebel – answer me, please!"

I try to answer, but I can't. My neck is locked in

place, and I can't speak. I feel like my head is going to be ripped off my shoulders.

It's my neckerchief – it's caught on the branch of a tree. It must have snagged when I crashed through the canopy, and stopped me hitting the ground. My back paws just about reach the branch beneath it, saving me from choking, but I don't have the strength to stay like this for much longer.

Jaxon can see what's happened. "Don't move! I'm going to get you down!"

As if I could move – my body feels dead, like cold clay. All I can do is hang and hurt. Jaxon's hurt too – his fur is coated in patches of blood – but it's not stopping him. He limps to the tree trunk and scrambles onto the lower branches. Then he climbs up, branch by branch, until he's reached the one that I'm hanging from.

"Stay steady," he orders.

He inches his body along the branch, making it sway and bob. Then he grips the scruff of my neck with his teeth and carefully unsnags my neckerchief. Grasping my fur tightly between his jaws, Jaxon shuffles himself backwards to the trunk, shuddering with effort, and slowly, painfully, climbs back down until he can lower me gently to the ground.

"There. That's it. You're safe, Rebel!"

I don't feel safe. I can feel every tender place where I struck a branch on the way down. I look up blearily.

"You're bleeding," I murmur.

"It's not my blood," he says. "I fought off most of the wolves so they couldn't follow you, and then the rest ran away when you pushed their leader off the cliff. I can't believe you did that, Rebel!" He laughs. "And now look at you – saved by your stupid neckerchief!"

I try to laugh with him, but I can't. My whole body is in agony. I feel like I've been sculpted from solid pain.

"Jaxon," I say. "I met the Companion. They took me to a cornfield. It was so beautiful."

Jaxon's laughter fades. He looks frightened all of a sudden.

"It's OK," he whispers. "I've got you. I've got you, Rebel."

He lifts me as gently as he can by the scruff of the neck and carries me through the forest. I watch the trees sway past, my head swimming. It all feels like it's happening to someone else.

Jaxon finds a hollow trunk lying on the forest floor. It's dark and damp inside, filled with the warm rotting scent of must. He carefully places me at the end.

"Here!" he says. "This'll do, won't it, Rebel?"

I don't even have the strength to answer him. Jaxon stares at me. There's something in his eyes that looks like fear. He wasn't scared of the wolves, and he wasn't scared to scramble down a sheer cliff face, but he's scared now. I don't know how I feel about that.

"OK," he says. "Don't worry. I'll make it nicer for you."

He limps outside, and comes back with mouthfuls of dry leaves. He starts piling them around me.

"See? Just like a human bed." He paws at the leaves, arranging them. "I'll bring you some water too, and something to eat. Maybe when you're feeling strong enough, we can play chase, and throw sticks, and all those other things you like. Maybe I'll find a stream and give you a bath. You like baths, don't you?"

I peer up at him weakly. "Jaxon, you don't have to do this."

I swallow. It's hard to talk, but I need to say it.

"You saved my life – twice. You knocked that wolf off me, and you got me down from the tree. Your debt's been repaid. You don't have to stay with me any longer."

Jaxon doesn't say anything for a while. He lies down beside me and pushes more leaves into place.

"Get some rest," he says quietly. "We'll talk when you're feeling better."

I do as he says, because I'm a good dog. Something is trying to drag me down, into a dark and secret place beneath the world; I keep bobbing out of it and then sinking back down again, deeper each time, until finally I give in and close my eyes, and let sleep carry me into the dark.

28
DAWN

I float between sleep and waking, in and out, like the moon passing behind clouds.

Sometimes, when I open my eyes, it's night; sometimes I open them and it's raining. The world outside the log seems a million miles away; inside feels all still and muffled and calm. It's like I'm lying at the bottom of a well, gazing up, watching sunlight ripple the water above me.

The only thing that stays the same is Jaxon. He brings me food; he licks my fur clean; he sleeps beside me to keep me warm. He's always there. I can't work out why he's doing it. I can't work out why he doesn't just leave.

Then one day, I open my eyes … and things are different.

It's morning. The air is cool and quiet. Jaxon is asleep beside me, his breathing as close as if it's my own. Every sound that reaches me is bright and clear and vivid: it feels like the first day that's ever been made.

I feel better. I get to my feet and limp out of the log; I can walk, but I'm sore all over. After so long being asleep – a day? Two days? A week? – the feeling of being outside again is overwhelming. I can smell *everything*: every plant, every leaf, every animal that's passed through the forest. I can even smell the sunlight on the grass, the air dancing down from the mountains, the—

I freeze. I can't believe what I'm seeing.

"Jaxon! *Jaxon!*"

There's a heavy *thump* from inside the log as Jaxon snaps awake and whacks his head on the ceiling. He comes scrambling out.

"Rebel! You're up! When did you—"

"Look!"

I'm facing the horizon. In front of us, a field curls down into a valley before meeting a wall of mountain ridge, rising sharply to the sky. And on the other side of that ridge…

A white tower. I know that tower. It's the one that Tom's been drawing in his sketchpad, over and over again.

"That's the tallest tower of the High Castle," I cry. "We've made it! We've been right beside the gorge the whole time, and we didn't even realize!"

Suddenly I don't feel weak any more. After all that I've been through, I'm finally going to see Tom again! I start to race down the hill as fast as I can.

"Come on!" I shout. "The Reds could be marching on the High Castle right now! We have to find Tom before—"

I stop mid-run. I can't believe I've been so stupid.

"You knew," I say, turning back to Jaxon. "You knew that we were this close, the whole time. Why didn't you wake me up and tell me?"

Jaxon meets my gaze for a moment. Then he slowly sits down, like his whole body is heavy with a weight he's been secretly carrying for days.

"Rebel," he says. "He isn't going to listen to you."

His voice sounds different. There's a softness to it that I haven't heard before.

"Tom isn't going to come home just because you want him to. He won't care about what you've done. He won't even understand. He's going to break your heart, just like all humans do, and he won't think twice about it."

I can feel myself flushing with anger. "Stop talking about Tom like that. You don't know anything about him!"

"Maybe I don't," says Jaxon, standing up. "But I know what I see, right in front of me. I see a dog who loves so much that he can't see the truth. I see a dog who cares so much about losing something that he'll die to get it back. I see a dog who's prepared to do everything, *anything*, for someone who doesn't care about him. And it breaks my heart, Rebel."

This isn't like the argument we had on the mountain. Back then, Jaxon was like a rock, cold and hard and impenetrable; now it's like something has broken right through him, revealing a vein of sadness hidden in the stone.

"No matter what you do, Tom will never listen. He will do as he likes. He will leave you, again and again, just like he left you the first time." He swallows. "But *I* won't leave you, Rebel."

And there it is. There's the reason why Jaxon has been so angry all this time; why he stuck beside me, even when he didn't have to. I've always thought that Jaxon was helping me because of his Masterless code. But now I understand it's much more than that. It all feels so clear and obvious that I can't believe I didn't see it.

Jaxon keeps going, stumbling over his words, determined to finish what he's started.

"You don't have to follow him. Tom can live his life, and you can live yours. With *me*. We can be one another's companion. We can spend the rest of our days together, just the two of us, safe and free in the mountains. We can be happy, Rebel. I know we can."

I shake my head. "I can't leave him, Jaxon."

"He left you."

"It's not the same."

"Yes, it is!" Jaxon takes a step towards me. "You were born free, Rebel. You don't belong to anyone. You don't have to come just because Tom calls you!"

"But he *didn't* call me!" I argue. "He never even asked me to follow him. He *told* me not to, Jaxon."

"Then why are you doing it?"

"Because…" I fumble for the words. "Because that's what love is. It pins you to things. It makes you do things that aren't right or clever or sensible, because you're not doing them for you. And that's exactly what makes them important. Because if you haven't got something outside of yourself to love, then you might as well be nothing."

Jaxon stares at me. The gap between us suddenly feels like it's opened wider, though neither of us has moved an inch.

"So you're choosing him."

"It's not like that. It's not one or the other. You can come too." The thought lights up a sudden blaze of hope inside me. "You could live with us on the farm! Tom would like you, he really would. You'd like him too, I think…"

But I look at Jaxon and see something on his face that I can't put into words, however hard I try. It's a part of him I've never seen before, one that I don't understand. It almost scares me a little. But he's not angry at me; he's so, so sad.

"I can't do that, Rebel," he says quietly.

So that's it. The blaze of hope inside me dies as quickly as it came, leaving only cold ash. Jaxon stands before the forest; I stand before the castle. We've both made our choices.

"I'm sorry, Jaxon," I say. "Thank you. For everything you've done for me. I'll never forget you."

I wait for him to say something back, but he doesn't. He doesn't need to – it's all right there, in that hopeless look on his face, even worse than the look he gave me in the cave, when he was bent double with pain and fear. He's hurting even more now.

"Goodbye, Jaxon."

I turn and run. At one point I look behind me and Jaxon is still there, still in the same spot where I left him. From this far away, he's no bigger than a dot on the landscape, and I wonder if he's already left and my eyes are playing tricks on me. But I can't tell, because they're too full of tears to be sure of anything any more.

THE
LAST
DAY

29

CAMP

I keep running down to the valley below me. I'm close enough to see tents now – and not just a few of them, either. There are hundreds, campfires and wagons too, all decked with red flags. This must be where the Reds have made camp before marching on the High Castle – I've made it just in time!

The thought that Tom is close makes me run even faster. And the faster I run, the more the wind dries my tears. I'm going to see Tom again. When he discovers that I've come all this way to find him, and realizes how much I love him, I know he won't want to fight any more. He'll leave it all behind, Rider and the Reds and the King, and the two of us will head back home together. Then it'll be just us again, the way it's meant to be. The hope of it makes my heart swell like the sun.

The smell of the camp dances on the wind towards me: food and fire and humans and horse dung, all mixed together. The Reds must have been here for a while. That makes sense – Jaxon and I lost two days up in the mountains, and I have no idea how long I was asleep for in the forest. But why are they waiting here? They're right beside the High Castle – don't they want to attack before the King tries to fight back?

Then I notice another smell in the air… A smell I recognize from Unsk after the explosion. It's fear and hate and desperation, hanging over the ground like fog. And it's *everywhere.*

I reach the tents, and I don't need to smell it any more – I can see it. It's pressed into the faces of the women, leaning at their tents like hung rags. It's there in the bodies of the elderly, hunched over campfires in worn blankets. It's in the eyes of the children who are pacing the camp in miserable silence.

There's no sign of Tom; there's no sign of Rider. The camp is almost empty. The ground is so trampled that there should be *thousands* of people here, but there aren't. What's going on? Where are the Reds?

"Well! Talk about a sight for sore eyes."

I spin around, and find myself staring up into a long, familiar face. "Pearl!"

The donkey from Unsk is tied to a post beside a tent. The cuts on her side are looking better, but she still has the bandage covering one eye. I can't see Felix with her.

"Poor mite wouldn't leave Unsk," Pearl sighs, reading my mind. "I tried my best to bring him with me, but he kept saying that he had to stay, in case his wife came back." She lets out a long huffle. "I've been on my hooves ever since! *Thousands* of people leaving Unsk, there were, so there was no rest for an old donkey like me. Carting this here, carting that there, standing outside in all weathers… They didn't even pack my blue blanket! I've a mind to complain, you know."

I gaze around the empty camp, panic seeping into me like damp mud. There's no sign of the thousands of people Pearl has mentioned.

"Where *is* everyone?"

She nods to the distance. "You've missed them, dearie. They went that way hours ago."

There's a path in the field beside us, churned to mulch by thousands of marching feet. It leads right up to the mountain ridge: there the rock wall splits like a set of bone jaws and forms a thin tunnel into the mountain. That's the gorge that leads to the High Castle. There's a sudden belt of wind from inside, carrying a sound from the belly of the gorge and sending it across the field towards us. The blare of horns, the crack of rifles, the cries of men.

"Thousands went in, all with pitchforks and spears," says Pearl darkly, "and no one's come back since."

I feel dread hollowing out my chest. The final fight has already begun.

I'm too late.

I'm running before I can stop myself, flying across the churned mud towards the jaws of the mountain.

"Rebel, no!" Pearl cries after me. "It's not safe!"

I know it isn't. If I enter that gorge, I might never come out again.

But that's always been the rule: wherever Tom goes,

I go too. I'm his dog and he's my boy. And if he's stepped right inside the jaws of death … then I'm going to follow him into them and bring him back out.

30
GORGE

I reach the entrance to the gorge. Inside is a thin corridor of dead earth and cold stone, bound by walls so tall they seem to scrape the gunmetal clouds above me. No sunlight touches the ground here; the gorge is filled with grim shadow and shifting smoke, so I can't make out what lies ahead.

But I can hear it. The sound of war is even louder now, rising on the breeze that blows towards me. Thousands of people bellowing at once, pierced with gunshots and sudden screams. With every trembling step I take, the noise grows louder and louder, drumming off the walls of the gorge. Terror pounds through me like snake venom. I have no idea what I'm going to find when I make it through the smoke.

Oh, Tom, please be safe…

Another belt of wind whips through the gorge, and the smoke clears. I'm standing at the top of a slope; beneath me, the gorge flattens out to a wide plain.

And there, right in front of me, is the High Castle.

It's even more beautiful than in Tom's drawings. A golden flag is sailing from the very top of the tallest tower, stretching high above the battle. The High Castle sits at the far end of the gorge, filling it from side to side, its walls as strong and thick as the mountain they're carved into. There's no way you can get around it: the only way in is through a huge gateway at the front, which is blocked by hundreds of guardsmen. There are more than I've ever seen before, lined up outside the castle walls in golden armour and aiming their muskets at the crowds ahead.

And as for those crowds…

They fill the gorge from edge to edge, like a churning sea. Thousands of Reds, all carrying home-made weapons and waving flags and roaring at the top of their lungs. The sound is huge, terrifying, a monster in itself, bellowing as one over the gunfire that seems to come from everywhere. The guardsmen are firing at the people, trying to drive them back as fast as they can reload, filling the gorge with smoke and screams, but the Reds keep pushing forward, thousands of boots grinding into the ground at the same time as they heave towards the High Castle in a crush...

I feel a bolt of horror. Tom is somewhere in that crowd. *"Tom!"*

I fly down the slope, racing into the sea of legs. I weave frantically through them, searching for any sign of Tom, but it's hopeless. There's too many voices, too many faces, too much noise. The air is rent with jagged howls of pain and pulsing with smoke. How will I find Tom in all this chaos?

I see a boulder jutting out of the ground in front of me – and suddenly I know what to do. I run and clamber on top of it, just like I did in the river. Finally I can see over the heads of the crowds.

The High Castle is in front of me, closer than before. The Reds are almost at the castle gates; the guardsmen might have better weapons and better training, but even their muskets can't hold back a crowd of thousands.

Every time they stop to reload, the Reds surge forward again, driving them back with spears and pitchforks. I see huge wooden ladders are being passed over the crowd to the front, and I suddenly understand what's happening – the Reds are going to try to scale the castle walls to get inside. Even if the gates are closed, there won't be anything to keep the Reds out.

There's another surge forward and the guardsmen on the battlefield are overrun. They turn and flee into the castle, pouring through the gates as fast as they can. The Reds roar with triumph and charge after them, holding their flags and ladders high above their heads…

BOOM!

The sound is so loud, so enormous, that it seems to silence the world. There's a flash of light from the castle walls, a plume of belching smoke. Something sails through the air, rippling like a growl as it flies towards the charging Reds…

CRASH! A cannonball bounces wildly off the battlefield, blasting rubble in an explosion and pinwheeling into the crowd. There's a scream of pain, a moment of stunned horror … and then more explosions, one after the other, as cannonball after cannonball is blasted from the High Castle.

I don't believe it. The King is firing cannons at his own people.

Screaming in terror, the Reds turn and run from the walls, dropping their ladders in their panic to escape the cannon fire. But there's nowhere to hide in the gorge, nowhere to flee except out through the tight bottleneck they came through. Within moments, the crowd at the exit has become a crush. They're trapped.

The ground in front of me suddenly shatters in a cloud of dust; a cannonball spins wildly past me, hitting the rock wall and unleashing an avalanche of rubble. I yelp in fright and fling myself from the boulder, racing back through the terrified crowds and twisting between their legs to try to get away. This is nothing like the posters that Tom drew: there's no sunrise here, no peace, no triumph, just chaos.

I gaze back across the battlefield, and my heart sinks. The red flags have been dropped and trampled into the dust. The ground is cratered and littered with lifeless bodies. There are injured people too, screaming with pain and pleading for others to help them, but no one can help, not without running back into the path of the cannon.

"*Come on!* We can't give up now!"

I recognize that voice. I turn around – and there, standing on the battlefield beside me, is Rider. He's bleeding from his head and holding up a rifle, still wearing his wolfskin.

"We have to keep fighting!" he roars at the crowds around him. "We're all that stands between the King and a free country! If we give up now, it's over!"

But no one's listening to him. The people are terrified – they know there's no way they can win against cannon, when all they have are handmade weapons and a few guns.

The battle is lost. The uprising has failed. I watch Rider hopelessly shouting at his terrified soldiers as they flee from the gorge ... and that's when I realize.

Rider is alone. Tom isn't with him.

Dread seeps through me. Tom's always been right by Rider's side in every drawing he's made. But he's not here now.

He's nowhere to be seen.

"Tom? Tom!"

Where is he? Is he one of those bodies lying broken on the battlefield? I look around frantically, trying to find him in the chaos, searching for some sign, some hope, some *anything*…

And then I see him.

I almost can't believe it at first. It's just a single small movement in the distance.

I blink the dust out of my eyes and look again. A boy, sprawled on the battlefield. Scruffy brown hair pasted over his eyes. A small, fast-breathing chest.

Tom.

He's flat on his back in a crater, right beside the castle gates. He must have been at the very front of the charge when the first cannonball hit. He's alive!

But he's hurt – badly. Blood is staining the ground around him and soaking through his trousers. He has just enough shelter to hide from the guardsmen on the castle walls, but no one can reach him without being shot themselves. He's trapped.

I run to Rider, leaping up at him and barking.

"Quick! You have to go back and save Tom!"

But Rider isn't listening to me – he's too busy shouting at the fleeing crowds as they run for their lives. I chase after them, barking desperately.

"No! Don't run! You have to stay and fight! If you don't, Tom will die!"

But no one understands me. No one even notices me. Jaxon was right: I'm just a dog in a human's world. No one cares that I'm about to lose the one person I've ever loved.

Tom is going to die.

I turn back to the battlefield, my eyes filling with tears, and I howl. Tom's so far away from me, so tiny, so lost. He looks just like *I* did when he rescued me as a puppy. He saved me, but I can't save him. No one will be with him when he dies. There will be no one to hold his hand in his last moments; no one to tell him that it's OK; no one to lie beside him and let him know how much he is loved.

Except me.

I stand and face the castle. I can see guardsmen lining the walls through the smoke, their muskets and cannon ready to strike down anything that moves on the battlefield.

I understand what I have to do. I know why I'm here. I can't bring Tom home. I can't save him.

But I can make sure he's not alone.

That's all that matters. I will be with Tom, and make sure he knows that I came to find him, even when he didn't call. That I tried to save him, even if I failed. That no matter how frightened he feels or how much he hurts, he is not alone. He has never been alone. He has always been loved.

And if I have to die for that to happen, then so be it.

I feel it straight away: my True Dog, alive and awake inside me. The part of me that's still wild, the part of me that's still free, the part of me that can stand against a wolf and win. My True Dog has led me here, to the person I love, and now it's sending me straight into the jaws of death to be with him one last time.

Because I am Rebel, and *I* get to decide what I do with my one and only life. And if I use it for anything, I'm going to use it for love.

I shut my eyes, hold my terror close, and charge.

31

CHARGE

I scramble over the stony ground. I'm the only thing that's moving on the battlefield now: one tiny dog in a valley of death. The High Castle looms through the smoke ahead, growing taller and clearer as I draw closer…

Bang!

The ground beside me erupts in shards of stone. The guardsmen are shooting at me, musket balls missing me by inches. I yelp with fear but keep running, my eyes fixed on Tom to give me courage. I can't stop now.

"I'm coming, Tom!" I cry.

The guardsmen stop firing at me – maybe because they're reloading, or maybe because they've realized I'm just a dog.

"Hey!" I hear someone shout behind me. "Look at that!"

I glance over my shoulder. Some of the Reds have stopped retreating and they're pointing at me as I race towards the castle.

"What is it doing?"

"It must be mad!"

"It's going to get killed…"

There's another *crack* from the castle, then another and another; the ground around me explodes with dust again, the musket balls whizzing past me like wasps. I don't stop; I keep running with everything I have, crossing the battlefield as thousands of Reds turn to watch me.

"Shooting at a dog!"

"The *monsters*…"

"But look! Look at what it's wearing!"

It takes me a moment to understand what they're talking about. It's my neckerchief – the one that Tom gave me. It's dirty and ragged and torn, almost hanging from my neck, but it's still there. I'm still wearing it, after all I've been through.

"It's charging!"

"Why?"

"It's never going to make it…"

But they're wrong. I *am* going to make it.

Up ahead, Tom is getting closer and closer. I don't care if I get shot. The Companion showed me what dying is, and I'm not frightened of it any more. All I care about is getting to Tom before it happens, so that we can be together one last time.

But I'm not just running for him now. I'm running for Jaxon. I'm running for Pearl. I'm running for Felix. I'm running for *all* the animals that I've met along the way, all the ones who've had no choice in this war but have still been made to suffer because of it, even the wolves. I'm running because it's our world too, and we should get to fight for what we care about, even if no one else cares.

And all of a sudden, I'm not running alone. Someone is racing across the battlefield beside me, his red flag held high.

"Come on!" cries Rider, his voice echoing boldly off the gorge walls. *"What are we waiting for? If he can do it, so can we!"*

There's a shout from behind us: more Reds are joining him, brandishing spears and pitchforks. It's just a dozen men and women, running towards a wall of death. It's hopeless.

But that's not how it feels. The air in the gorge has changed; the scent of despair has lifted. Something else is filling the space around me – the same feeling I sensed in Unsk when the crowds first saw Tom's poster. The feeling that maybe, just maybe, a new world is possible. That something amazing can happen, right here, right now, if we all fight for it. It spreads through the crowds like gorse fire, carried from one person to the next.

And all at once, the Reds have stopped retreating. They're turning back to the High Castle and charging. They're injured and bleeding, leaning on one another for support, their clothes covered in filth and dust, but they're fighting anyway. They've found their True Dog. They've stood between a wolf and a sheer drop and found the strength to survive. They pick up the flags from the ground, bloodied and ripped and charred at the edges, and hold them high once more.

"Let them hear us!" Rider shouts. *"Let them know we're coming! They can't take us all at once!"*

The Reds raise their voices and roar – and it's an animal roar that comes out of them, exhausted and alive all at once, a single steady note that fills the gorge from end to end and makes the air tremble. A sea of Reds is charging at the High Castle, a final push together as one. I never meant to lead a charge. I never meant for anyone to follow me. But if I have to win a war to save Tom, then so be it.

BOOM!

The walls erupt – the guardsmen have opened up their cannon again. The ground is hammered with cannonballs, sending up huge plumes of dust. I hear people scream with pain as they fall, feel a burst of shattered rock hail down around me, but it makes my True Dog rage inside me all the more. I can't die now. I won't die. I can't get this close to Tom and fail. I keep running.

So do the Reds. The tide of the battle has turned; not even the cannon can stop them now. They're picking up the ladders that were abandoned and carrying them to the castle walls. We're so close we can see the panic in the guardsmen's eyes as they frantically reload. In just a few moments, another volley of death will be unleashed against us. I might have only seconds to find Tom...

But where is he? I can't see him any more – the air is thick with blinding smoke. I raise my nose to find his scent, but all I can smell is blood and sulphur and scorched metal, filling the gorge around me...

And then I find it. A single scent, hidden beneath the fear and sweat and grease and gunpowder. A golden thread, hovering over the chaos of the battlefield. A smell I know as well as I know myself.

It's Tom – his hair, his clothes, the charcoal under his fingernails, the conkers in his pockets. It's more than his voice and his beating heart, more than his blood and his breathing. It's the part of him that's most truly him, the part he can't change, the glow that sits around him and makes him my home. I lift my head and run, following the scent like a river to the sea, winding through the slaughter and chaos as the High Castle rears ahead of me and the smoke parts like curtains in the wind.

And there he is. He's lying in the crater, bloody fingers gripping the ground in fear, his face pale and wet with tears. His clothes are ripped, and his eyes are swollen, and he's terrified … but the moment he sees me, the fear disappears like mist at sunrise. He's just a boy again, waking up on Sunday morning, all of him Tom.

"Rebel?" he cries.

"Tom!" I scream.

A hundred miles becomes a hundred feet and then ten feet and then nothing as I leap through the air and throw myself into his waiting arms. Trembling, Tom grips me close and doesn't let go. I bury my head in his embrace: my Tom, my boy, my everything. And finally, after all this time, after all this distance, in this terrible place a million miles away, it's just like it's always been. I've never felt more home, never in all my days.

The Reds charge past us like a flood, clearing the last of the battlefield and hitting the castle walls. In moments, I can hear them shouting at each other to raise the ladders, to climb the walls, to push back the guardsmen at the cannon, blowing their horns to call back the last of the retreating Reds.

Tom and I don't join them. We stay where we are, holding each other tight, love springing out of us like flowers. The others might as well not be there.

Where we are, there is no war.

32
VICTORY

The rest of the day is a blur.

I don't leave Tom's side, not once. The sound of shouts and gunfire slowly dies away, but I don't care if the battle is won or lost. In the crater, in Tom's arms, we have everything we need.

After what feels like hours, I hear people walking nearby. I bark to get their attention. Within moments, two Reds peer over the edge of the crater and gawp down at us.

"Hey, we've got another wounded one over here!"

"Oof – that leg doesn't look too good…"

"Come on, help me get him out."

They heave Tom out of the crater and carry him between them. I run after them, sticking so close to their heels that I keep tripping them up. I've just run through death itself to find Tom – I'm not losing him now.

They carry him through the castle gates, which are broken in half and hanging off their hinges. I can't believe my eyes when I step inside. The guardsmen are gone. Instead, the courtyard of the High Castle – every window, every balcony, every walkway and stairwell – is packed with Reds, cheering at the top of their lungs and pointing at the sky.

I look up. At the very top of the tallest tower, the golden flag of the King has been pulled down. A new flag is flying in the wind. A red flag.

The King has been defeated. The High Castle is theirs. After years of suffering, the country is finally free.

At that moment, Rider marches out of the main castle keep, flanked by armed Reds. It's clear that he's in charge here: he holds up his hands, and everyone falls silent immediately. Rider gazes around, taking them all in.

"The King's escaped," he announces. "We've just found a secret tunnel in the dungeons that leads out through the mountains. The coward fled during the final attack, and left his men to die!"

A handful of guardsmen are dragged into the courtyard with their hands aloft, trapped in a ring of raised guns. They look terrified. The Reds jeer at them, shouting insults and shoving them from all sides. Then suddenly the mood turns and the crowd surges forward, weapons in their hands and hate in their eyes...

Rider leaps in front of the guardsmen, shoving people back. "*No!* Don't touch them! They're our prisoners!"

"Prisoners?" someone near the front shouts. "You want to let them live, after what they've done to us?"

"For pity's sake," says Rider, his voice heavy with exhaustion. "Look at them. They're just boys."

And he's right. With their helmets off, everyone can see the guardsmen are just frightened young men, barely filling the armour they've been made to wear. They look like Tom.

Rider points at them. "Where do you think the King recruited them? They're *your* boys. They're *your* countrymen. The King might have turned them into monsters, but we won't let him do the same to us. This is a new country!"

People are still trying to argue with him, but they're silenced by another shout.

"Hey – look!"

Everyone turns. A woman is pointing at me, beaming from ear to ear.

"That's him!" she shouts. "The dog that led the charge!"

She picks me up and holds me above the crowd, and the argument is instantly forgotten. Everyone's far too busy cheering for me. Then they all start jostling one another so they can get close enough to pat my head and tickle my chin and ruffle my fur.

"What a hero!"

"If he hadn't run when he did…"

"Such a clever dog!"

"Good boy! That's a good boy!"

My tail wags. I *am* a good boy.

The woman puts me gently back beside Tom's feet. "Is he yours?"

Tom raises his head weakly, and smiles. "His name's Rebel. And he's the best dog in the whole wide world."

The crowd gives the biggest cheer yet, and everyone moves aside so Tom can be carried into the castle. I follow close behind like his shadow. We're taken to a big room that's been hastily turned into a hospital for the injured. As the men try to find a free bed for Tom, a nurse stops them in their tracks.

"What are you doing?" she snaps, pointing at me. "Get *that* out of here!"

One of the men laughs. "Don't you know who this is? That dog's a hero!"

"And this is a hospital," says the nurse grimly. "I'm trying to save lives. You can't bring two dogs in here!"

That stops me in my tracks. *Two* dogs?

I spin around – and there, striding past the beds towards me, is…

"Jaxon!"

It's him, all right – and his face is like absolute thunder. Before I can say anything else, he knocks me to the ground.

"You're lucky you're still alive," he growls, "because if you weren't, I would absolutely kill you."

I blink. "What are you doing here?"

"What do you think?!" he roars. "Don't you remember the first thing I told you? I am beholden to dogs in trouble. And *you,* Rebel, manage to get in more trouble than any dog I've ever known. Running across that battlefield! How can I not follow you, when you keep doing *stupid* things like that?"

I'm so happy I think I might explode. I run in circles around Jaxon, jumping up and licking his face. "You came back for me!"

The nurse finally loses her temper. "That's it! Get them out of here, before—"

She tries to grab me, but Jaxon snaps at her ferociously. The nurse runs away with a squeak, and that's the end of that – no one dares touch me now. Tom is led shakily to a bed and lowered onto the mattress. I climb up onto the cold crisp sheets beside him and Jaxon stands guard at the end of the bed. We're finally back where we started – Tom and I, lying together.

He gazes at me through weak eyes. "Can you believe it, Rebel? The High Castle. We did it."

My tail wags. I don't care about the High Castle – all I've ever cared about is Tom. I want to tell him everything

I've been through to find him: all the adventures I've had, and the people and animals I've met, Jaxon and Felix and Pearl and Pol and Grandad and the wolves and the Companion … but I can't say any of that, of course, because I'm a dog.

Tom strokes my head, and his eyes suddenly darken. "I thought I was going to die on that battlefield," he whispers. "A cannonball hit the ground right beside me. All I could do was lie in that crater and think about you, and Mum, and Dad … how I'd never see any of you again. I told myself that if I made it out alive, I'd come straight back home and find you and never leave." He smiles. "But you found *me*, Rebel. You came all this way for me. I missed you so much."

All of a sudden, my joy disappears, like the sun behind clouds. All the sadness I've held inside me for days on end – all my fear, all my hurt – comes pouring out of me at once.

If you've missed me so much, then why did you leave me? I want to shout at him. *Why didn't you come back? Why did you forget about me?*

Everything that Jaxon said is true. Tom left me

behind. He stopped drawing me. How can we be together like we were before, when I know how easy it was for him to forget me?

The nurse finally plucks up the courage to approach the bed again, keeping a wary eye on Jaxon. "Come on," she orders the volunteers hovering beside her. "Sit him up, so we can check his injuries."

Tom sits up weakly as the soldier removes his clothes, and I see that there's something hidden underneath his shirt. A sheet of paper. No, not just one sheet – dozens of them, old and worn and ripped, stained with mud and sweat and stuffed inside his clothes.

"What on *earth*..." says the soldier.

He pulls out a sheet, holds it up – and there I am. Me, sketched in charcoal. The soldier pulls out another, and there's me again, curled up in the blankets on the bed. Me, begging for food under Tom's chair. Me, running through the grass in Top Field. Me and Tom, watching the clouds pass by. Me and him and him and me, page after page, over and over again, dozens of drawings spilling out of him.

And there's the truth, shining in front of me like

the sun. Tom's never stopped drawing me. He's never forgotten me. He's been thinking about me the whole time, just like I've been thinking about him. But instead of sticking those drawings on doors and noticeboards, he's kept them pressed close to his heart, secret and safe, so he would always have them with him.

I rest my head against his side, and he holds me until we fall asleep. We've never needed words before, and we don't need them now. We've already said everything we need to say.

THE
NEW
DAYS

33

THRONE

*T*om spends the next two days in bed. Lots of people come to visit him: people he's been marching with, but strangers too. They want to meet me and see "the rebel dog" for themselves. Whenever it seems like Tom is getting tired, Jaxon starts growling at them, and they leave pretty quickly after that. Tom's grateful for it, even though he still has no idea who Jaxon is, and I can tell he finds it all a bit confusing.

Then one morning, a Red walks in and summons him upstairs. He doesn't explain why, and Tom doesn't ask. He's well enough to walk now, so he limps out of bed and Jaxon and I follow him along the castle's corridors. It's strange, walking on something so flat and smooth and man-made after days of mud and rocks.

The man leads us up endless stairways, until we finally come to a set of double doors guarded by more men with guns. They stand aside for Tom as he limps past, and Jaxon and I follow him inside.

My mouth drops open. I've never seen a room so big or grand before. Stained glass windows cast pools of rainbow light across the floor; the ceiling is encrusted with jewels and held aloft by marble columns that are broader than trees. A set of steps at the far end leads to a gleaming golden throne.

Sitting on the steps in front of it, eating an apple, is a man wearing a wolfskin.

The hair on my back goes up. It's Rider – the man who took Tom away from me. The man who led him onto a battlefield, and left him to die in a crater. I hate him with everything I have.

"Ah! Back on your feet already!" exclaims Rider, chucking away the apple core and striding towards Tom. "You must heal quickly. Not bad for a twelve-year-old."

Tom opens his mouth to answer, then blushes furiously. Rider cuffs him around the ear. I bark with fury. How dare he hit Tom!

"*That's* for lying to me," Rider growls. "*Sixteen?* If I'd known the truth, I'd have *never* let you join the Reds. Now look at you!" He points at Tom's leg. "That injury's going to stay with you for the rest of your life."

Tom swallows. "I'm sorry. I didn't mean to lie. I just wanted to help stop the King."

Rider sighs. "Well, you did. And now here you are, in his very own throne room." He holds out his hands to the walls of gleaming gold. "Not bad, eh?"

"It's beautiful," says Tom.

Rider shrugs. "We'll melt it all down and sell it. We'll need it to pay for the rest of the war."

Tom blinks. "But … the war's over. We won."

Rider shakes his head grimly. "The war's far from over, boy. The King's still somewhere out there, and there are plenty of guardsmen on the run who are still loyal to him. No doubt the King'll rebuild his army and try to take back the High Castle. There's going to be lots more fighting before this country is finally free."

Tom looks confused. It doesn't sound like the victory he thought it would be. It's nothing like the one in his drawings.

"I'm not sure I have the stomach left for any of it myself," continues Rider bitterly. "I've sent a lot of good people to their deaths. I almost sent *you* to your death, remember." He sighs again. "But I can't let those people have died for nothing. I have to keep fighting, to make it all worth it. That's the price I have to pay." He places a hand on Tom's shoulder. "But not you, Tom. It's time you went home."

My tail wags – we're going home! I'm so happy I could burst.

But Tom doesn't look happy. He shifts the weight off his injured leg. "If you don't mind, sir … I'd like to stay. For a bit longer."

Rider frowns. "Don't tell me you want to see more fighting?"

"No!" says Tom quickly. "Not at all. I'm done with fighting, for ever. I miss my parents like mad; I want to go home and see them again, I really do. It's just…" He awkwardly shifts to his bad leg again. "There's nothing for me back there."

I'm stunned. How can Tom say that? How can he say that the farm is *nothing*?

"I don't want to be a farmer," Tom admits, his voice barely a whisper. "I don't think I ever did. And now I've seen a bit more of the world, it's made me realize it properly."

Rider nods to Tom's leg. "Hmm. Let's face it – with an injury like that, you'll never be able to run a farm anyway. So what *are* you going to do?"

"I can't do anything," Tom grumbles.

"Rubbish," scoffs Rider. "Those posters you made – they *meant* something to people, Tom. You have talent. You should see where that takes you."

Tom looks miserable. "I suppose I might be able to get a small drawing job in Connick…"

Rider smiles. "That doesn't sound like nothing to me, boy. You'd be back with your family, doing something you're good at, in a place that you love. People build their lives around things like that. It's what gets them up in the mornings and sends them to sleep each night. It's what brought all these thousands of people here. They didn't want to change the world. They were fighting for their homes and their families and their friends and the small nothings that make their days worthwhile.

Small nothings can move mountains, if you let them."

Tom scowls. "So that's it? The country's finally free, and I'm just going to go back home again?"

"That's right," says Rider firmly. "Because you choose it. That's what freedom is, isn't it? The freedom to choose."

He reaches out a hand for Tom to shake. It's just like when they first met, back at the farm, before all of this happened.

"Goodbye, Tom. Go and enjoy your life. Follow the path home, and see where it leads." He nods at me. "And treat your dog to something tasty. If it hadn't been for him, the whole battle might have had a very different outcome. A dog like that is one in a million."

My tail wags. I have decided that Rider is nice after all.

With that, Tom limps out of the room and I follow him. He doesn't look sad any more; there's a spark of something new in his eyes. He's just seen that a whole new world is possible. He's ready to go home.

I'm ready to go home too. But there's a funny feeling in my stomach. I always knew there were bits of the farm that Tom didn't like, but I didn't realize how unhappy he was. I had no idea he didn't want to be a farmer. I thought he just needed reminding how good everything was – after all, how could he be unhappy, when everything was so perfect?

But I realize now that it *wasn't* perfect. It can't have been, not if Tom was unhappy. I came all this way to make things go back to normal, but now I see that the plans I had for us, everything that I've fought for, won't work any more. Tom has changed; when we get back to the farm, everything else will have to change too. It can't be the same as it was. But I think that's going to be fine.

After all, I've changed too, haven't I?

34
WAGONS

Tom spends the rest of the day saying goodbye to people, and gathering the few items he brought with him. There's not much, of course – just some stubs of charcoal and his sketchpad, which looks even more worn and battered than he does. Then the three of us – me, Tom, Jaxon – make our way out of the High Castle and into the battlefield. I'm almost sad to leave it behind – after all, this is going to be the last time that the three of us are together.

The gorge is filled with wagons that have arrived from the camp, ready to take the injured back home along the mountain road. Tom limps between them, trying to find one with enough space for us.

"Rebel!"

I turn around – and there's Pearl, shackled to a nearby wagon. Her bandages are all off now, and her injured eye seems to be healing.

"There you are!" she says. "I've been looking *everywhere* for you!"

My tail wags. "You have?"

"To give you a piece of my mind," she snaps. "It's not polite, running away when you're in the middle of a conversation like that. And to do something so dangerous, too! Someone needs to teach you some manners."

My tail stops wagging. "Sorry."

"Apology accepted!" says Pearl cheerfully. "Truth is, I'm just glad to see you well. Now, hop aboard! We're heading back to Unsk. Back to my nice warm stable and my favourite blue blanket." She shivers with anticipated pleasure. "Gosh, I've missed that blanket. I can almost feel it now."

"Looks like your dog and my donkey have made friends," says a voice behind us.

I turn to see who's driving the wagon. It's Meg, the young girl who read out Tom's poster in Unsk.

"Rebel seems to make friends wherever he goes," says Tom, rubbing my head. "You're not going to Connick, are you?"

Meg shakes her head. "Just Unsk. But there's bound to be someone there who can take you further. Jump on — there's enough room for the dogs in the back too. Even the big one."

Tom glances at Jaxon. "Er … this one isn't mine, to be honest. I have no idea who he belongs to. But he can come along if he wants t—"

Jaxon leaps onto the wagon before Tom can finish the sentence. I blink at him.

"Jaxon? You're coming with us?"

He gives me a puzzled look. "Of course I am. How else am I supposed to get to your stupid farm?"

I'm about to tell Jaxon that it *isn't* stupid — but then I realize what he just said. "Wait — you're coming to the farm?"

Jaxon sighs. "I've been thinking about what you said — about love pinning you to things. I've lived by myself for a long time now. I've always answered to myself, and no one else … but I think it might be time

I was pinned to something. And if being pinned to you means being pinned to Tom and the farm, well, so be it."

My head is spinning. "But that means sleeping in a house. It means letting Mum and Dad feed you." I grimace. "They might even make you have a bath sometimes."

"Stop talking before I change my mind," he snaps.

I jump on board, licking Jaxon's face and yapping for joy. "This is the best day ever!"

Tom climbs up beside Meg, and the wagon moves on. We watch from the back as Pearl begins the steady, trundling route to Unsk, and the towers of the High Castle shrink behind us. I never thought I'd see it with my own eyes, and I know I'm probably never going to see it again. Part of me feels sad about that. But another, larger part of me is excited. We're going home. We have so many new adventures ahead, the three of us.

I sit down on a heap of straw beside me, and hear the smallest, politest of squeaks from inside. I jump up.

"Oh! Sorry! I didn't realize someone was in here."

A little dormouse pokes her head out of the straw. She looks exhausted.

"It's OK," she squeaks. "I was asleep. Are we moving again?"

"We're going to Unsk," I tell her.

Her eyes light up. "Oh, thank goodness! That's where I've been trying to get to! I've been so lost for so long…"

It hits me then, like an apple falling from a branch. "Your name isn't Beatrice, is it?"

She looks surprised. "How did you know?"

I smile. "I'm a friend of Felix. We've been helping him look for you. He's been worried sick."

Beatrice beams. "Oh! I'm so glad you've been helping him. Felix does get rather flustered sometimes." She sighs. "I never *meant* to get lost. But by the time I woke up and realized what was happening… Well, it was too late. I had to find somewhere safe to hide, so that nobody would find us."

I blink. "Us?"

Beatrice smiles, and moves to one side. There, tucked in a safe little nook of warm straw, is a tiny nest of wriggling baby mice.

* * *

On and on we go, me and Jaxon and Tom and Pearl and Meg and Beatrice and the babies, a happy little family in the wagon. We follow the road as it unwinds around the mountains like ribbon, a train of wagons in front and a train behind. By day, we watch the world slip past us; at night, the wagons gather together and everyone shares food and stories, until the canvas sheets roll down and we sleep as one beneath the stars.

Then, one morning, I realize I recognize the view outside the wagon. The river, the bridge, the houses…

"It's Unsk!" I cry.

My heart leaps. I can see that the streets are packed with people waving flags, cheering as the Reds are brought home. All around us families are reunited, returning heroes tackled to the ground by their brothers and sisters. Everywhere I look, I see tears being shed and children hugged closer than before. I keep my eyes peeled for Felix in the crowds.

And then I spot him – a tiny figure scurrying across the cobbles, darting between the herds of stamping feet. He looks desperate, zipping along the road as he searches every wagon he passes.

"Beatrice? My love? Are you in there?"

I watch in horror as he almost gets squashed twelve times in a row.

Jaxon belts off the wagon and flies towards him, grabbing Felix and carrying him back in his mouth. He spits him into the straw with a sorry shake of his head.

"If it wasn't for me," he mutters, "*everyone* in this wagon would be dead."

Felix jumps to his feet, disorientated and drenched in slobber. "W-what's going on? Get off me! Who do you think you—"

"Felix?"

He spins at the sound of Beatrice's voice, and gazes in disbelief and wonder. It's like watching a tiny flower open to the sun.

"Beatrice? My love?"

She grabs him tight and doesn't let go. "You came to find me! My big, brave mouse!"

Felix beams. "Where have you *been*? I've been so—"

He looks down and sees the nest of babies in the straw. He looks up at Beatrice, then back at the babies, and then at Beatrice again, then back at the babies. "Oh! I see. Goodness."

I sit at the back of the wagon with a glow in my chest, watching it all unfold before me. The whole town is filled with thousands of small nothings like that: the moments that Rider spoke about, the tiny joys that people fight for and make it all worth living. When you see this many together, all at once, you understand how big small nothings can be.

I glance over at Pearl. Meg has just come out of the stable with a blue blanket and placed it over her back. Pearl has her eyes closed, and her ears laid flat against her neck, and her eyelids are flickering with joy. I don't think I've ever seen anyone look so happy in all my life.

35
ROAD

We spend the night with Meg and her family, and the next morning searching for a wagon that's heading back through Drulter and Connick. It takes ages; the town is filled with people trying to find a way home, and almost all the wagons are full. The ones that *do* have space won't allow two dogs on board. We finally find one that will let us on, wave goodbye to Pearl and Felix and Beatrice and Meg, and continue with our journey.

It's not exactly comfortable. The wagon is packed, and the three of us are pressed tight against one another for mile after shuddering mile. Jaxon doesn't seem happy about it – he seems out of place somehow, crouched inside a wagon on a paved road. Whenever I look at him, he's gazing up to the point where the mountains touch the sky, and I can't work out the look on his face.

Tom doesn't seem happy, either. "I don't know if we'll find anywhere in Drulter to sleep tonight," he mutters, glancing at the crowds on the road beside us. "Everywhere's going to be packed. We might have to sleep outside."

He rubs his injured leg and winces. I lay my paw on his good leg, so he knows that whatever happens, he won't have to face the night alone. Then I try to keep myself occupied by gazing out of the back of the wagon and watching the world roll past...

And suddenly, I catch a smell I recognize. Old pickles and hot soup. I glance around, and sure enough, I see a familiar orange tuft poking from the ferns by the road.

"Seamus!"

The pig I saved in Connick is rooting around in the forest for acorns. I jump down from the wagon and run to him, tail wagging.

"Rebel, my lad!" cries Seamus, grunting happily when he sees me. "Well I never! What are you doing out here?"

"Heading back home!" I tell him. "What about you? How's freedom treating you?"

"Marvellous! Couldn't be better! All the acorns I can eat, and, er…"

He trails off. Seamus doesn't seem happy at all. Now that I think about it, he's looking much thinner than when I last saw him.

"Look, I'll be honest," he mutters. "There's nothing *wrong* with acorns, absolutely nothing at all. Better than being sold for sausages any old day! But … *gosh*, I miss pigswill. I really, really miss pigswill." He looks at me pleadingly. "You don't have any pigswill, do you?"

I shake my head. "Sorry."

Seamus sags. "Oh well. Never mind. Acorns it is, then."

I watch him pick miserably at the ground. This isn't right. I saved Seamus's life by letting him out of that cage; I thought that everything *after* that would be easy. But it turns out Seamus needs more than freedom to be happy: he needs food, and warmth, and people to look after him too.

I thought all of our problems would be over by

now – instead it seems like they're just beginning. How am I supposed to fix all this?

"Rebel!"

I glance over my shoulder. The wagon has stopped in the road; Tom is leaning out.

"What are you doing?" he shouts. "Come on! We need to get to Drulter before nightfall!"

And the answer appears in my head, like the flick of a shooting star.

"I've got it!"

We reach Drulter as the sun is beginning to set. The town is just as packed as Unsk was, filled with people stopping for the night as they journey home along the mountain road. The tavern is heaving. Tom climbs down from the wagon and gathers his things.

"Right," he sighs. "I've no idea how we're going to find somewhere to stay. Doing it with two dogs would have been bad enough … now I have to do it with two dogs and a *pig*!"

Seamus has followed us to Drulter, sticking close to our wagon. It's all part of my brilliant plan, and now the final part is coming into play. I've just spotted a familiar dog, snuffling through the tavern crowd beside us.

"Hello, friends!" says Rollo, gazing up at the punters with a waggy tail and greedy eyes. "So wonderful to see you! I'm ever so hungry, so if you happen to have any spare chips…"

"Ahem."

Rollo turns around and stares straight into the cold, murderous eyes of Jaxon. I've never seen a dog shrink so fast in my life.

"F-f-friend!" he squeals in terror. "H-h-how n-n-nice to see y—"

"Enough!" Jaxon snarls. "You tried to sell us out for a handful of food. I should break every treacherous bone in your body."

Rollo backs away, trembling all over. "P-please! It was a mistake! I'll do *anything…*"

"That's right," Jaxon snaps. "You'll stay right here and keep your mouth shut. If you try to spoil anything, I'll rip your throat out." He gives me the nod. "All yours, Rebel."

I turn to Seamus. "You ready?"

Seamus knows exactly what to do – he's a born performer. He trots up to the customers outside the tavern and starts snuffling at their feet, oinking cheerfully and flapping his ears.

"Greetings, friends! Splendid to see you! Say, you wouldn't happen to have any chips going spare?"

The customers love it – I knew they would. They all stop what they're doing and point at Seamus, chuckling. Within seconds, they're throwing chips for him. Seamus scoffs them straight off the pavement, delighted.

"This is disgusting," mutters Jaxon, shaking his head. "You're turning him into a spectacle!"

"I think Seamus quite likes being a spectacle," I point out.

He does. He's in his element, performing a victory lap through the crowd as chips rain down around him. Even the tavern owner has stepped outside to watch, standing beside Tom.

"Well I never," he marvels. "He yours?"

Tom is baffled. "Er … I think so, yeah."

The tavern owner nods thoughtfully. "Hmm. I've always wanted a pub pig. The locals seem to like him too. He'll make me a fortune in chips." He turns to Tom. "I'll make you an offer. Give me that pig, and I'll clear out a back room for you to stay in tonight. I'll even throw in some food for your dogs."

Jaxon's head whips around. I can see a flash of something in his eyes – disgust, shame, anger. He doesn't like being called *Tom's dog*.

But I'm delighted. Everything has come together perfectly. Tom's got somewhere to sleep, Jaxon and I have something to eat, and Seamus has a place to stay for life. The only one who isn't happy is Rollo.

"That's not fair!" he howls. "That pig's going to take all my food! I haven't got a chance with him around…"

"Shut up!" Jaxon snarls. "You've still got regular meals, and somewhere to sleep. That's more than most dogs have, and more than you deserve!"

We spend the night in a cosy room at the top of the tavern. Through the window, I can see Seamus slumped on a pile of straw in the stables, sleeping off the biggest meal he's had in days. He takes up so much room that Rollo has to sit outside in the rain, whining pitifully.

The tavern owner has made Tom a little camp bed

to sleep on. The three of us curl up on it together. I've never been happier to be back on warm blankets, with those I love, but Jaxon can't get comfortable. He's not used to sleeping in a human bed. No matter where he lies, he can't seem to settle.

"Are you OK?" I ask him.

"I'll sleep on the floor," he mutters.

I watch as he lies down on the hard floorboards. Once again, I'm struck by how out of place Jaxon looks here. He doesn't belong in a room. It's like watching a left foot try to fit into a right shoe.

Later that night, I open my eyes, and see that Jaxon is wide awake. He's gazing out of the window, staring at the point where the stars touch the mountains. The rain has stopped now, and the sky is clear. Far in the distance, a thousand different animals are calling, weaving a song of midnight wildness. Wind is making the treetops shiver and bristle like fur, and Jaxon's eyes are full of a hunger that no amount of food can satisfy.

36
RETURN

*T*he day begins exactly as it should.

We rise early and find another wagon, and set off along the final stretch to Connick. At first, we're with lots of other travellers; but slowly, with every passing crossroads, people peel off and the numbers dwindle. Soon it seems like our wagon is the only one left on this road.

We move much faster, now the wagon is carrying fewer people. Mile by mile, path by path, I can taste the air changing around us. The scent of the wide world is becoming the scent of *home* again. The grass, the pine, the moisture in the air as it sinks down from the mountains … it's all just as I remember. My heart sings as I breathe it in. I had no idea how much I've missed that smell.

Jaxon still doesn't seem as happy, though. He gazes out of the back in silence, watching the mountains get smaller and smaller behind us.

Finally, just before the day is out, we arrive back in Connick. It's strange, seeing it again. It seemed so big to me the first time I saw it; now it almost looks small. Tom climbs down carefully on his injured leg, and the wagon moves on without us.

Tom turns to face the road, setting his jaw. I know he's worried about what Mum and Dad will say when he arrives home. He'll have a lot to explain to them, and a lot to apologize for. It's going to be a big shock for Mum and Dad when they find out that Tom doesn't want to be a farmer.

But I have a feeling it'll be OK. When Tom comes home safe and well, Mum and Dad will be so happy to have him back that they won't mind a thing. Besides, Tom's done a lot of brave things lately.

"Come on, boys," he sighs. "Time to go home."

He starts to limp down the road, and Jaxon sticks close beside him. But I don't. I stay right where I am.

Tom turns around. "Rebel? Are you coming?"

I don't move.

Jaxon turns around too. "Rebel, come on."

"This isn't going to work, Jaxon," I say quietly.

Tom glances at us, confused.

Jaxon shifts on his paws. "Stop messing around. The farm's this way."

"I know it is," I say. "But you're not coming with us."

Jaxon frowns. "Of course I'm coming with you!"

"No, you're not. You know as well as I do that you don't belong there. You're not a farm dog, Jaxon. You never will be."

Jaxon sits down, and is silent for a moment. "You don't want me there."

I shake my head. "I *do* want you there, more than anything. But this isn't about what I want any more. I can't make you change who you are, just so you can be with me. You can't be kept, Jaxon. You can't beg for food or sleep in a bed. It'd be like putting a bird in a cage or keeping a tree in the dark. I couldn't call myself a friend if I made you do it. I love you too much." I swallow. "And sometimes, loving something means letting it be where it belongs."

Tom is watching us closely. Jaxon sags where he sits. He knows I'm right. But his eyes are pleading and scared, like they were back in the cave. "I can't be alone for the rest of my life, Rebel. You were right about that."

"Then don't be," I say.

I walk over and sit beside him, so that we're facing the mountains together, side by side.

"There's a path over there, between those two houses. It leads up to the sheep trails. Follow that, and you'll find the place where we first met each other. Follow the path back to Unsk and cut across the wilderness – climb the mountain. Find your way back to Pol and her grandad, and live with them."

Jaxon glances at me. "With a *master*?"

"With friends," I say. "They won't try to keep you. They'll let you be your own dog. You can spend your days in the wild, and come back to them when you need to. You'll have the freedom to choose. *That's* where you belong, Jaxon."

There's another silence between us – but it's a different silence now, a living one, filled with words that don't need to be said. The fear in Jaxon's eyes has gone; he's sitting up straight again. It's like he's spent the last few days weighed down with chains, and he's finally free of them.

He stands up slowly, and walks to where Tom is waiting for us on the road. At first, I don't understand what he's doing. Then he leans forward and licks Tom's hand, just once.

"Take care of him," he says. "Please."

Then he walks back to me, and leans down to nuzzle me with his head. Jaxon's always been so much bigger than me; I never imagined that one day, he'd need me just as much as I've needed him, maybe even more.

"Goodbye, Rebel," he says gruffly. "I have a feeling we'll see each other again."

I think about the golden cornfield, and I know he is right.

I watch as he heads towards the point where the road meets the trail. He's almost out of sight when I call him a final time. "Jaxon?"

He turns around.

"You were always my companion," I say.

Jaxon smiles. And for the first time ever, I see his tail wag. "Mine too, Rebel."

He starts to run up the trail – slowly at first, and then sprinting up to the peak with everything he has in him. He doesn't look back as he goes – Jaxon never does. And as I watch him get faster and faster, I know that I was right to let him go. He's found his True Dog. He's back where he belongs. I watch him run until he's just a speck on the mountainside, and then the forest takes him back, and Jaxon is gone.

"Rebel?"

Tom is still standing on the road, waiting for me, gazing at the point where Jaxon disappeared.

"He was your friend, wasn't he?" He thinks for a moment, then looks at me. "You can go with him if you want. Or … would you rather stay?"

As if he needs to ask. I run to him, my Tom, my boy, and wrap myself around him. It's just the two of us again, after all this time. Tom smiles, and leans down to rub my tummy.

"Little Belly," he says softly.

The sun is behind us now, and the road before us is

golden in the light, spooling on towards home. We head down it together, side by side. Tom's limp is already healing, but I can see his leg is never going to be the same again. He's going to need time to recover. Which is good – Tom needs time. He needs time to remember what he left behind. He needs Mum and Dad and lamb stew and Top Field, and the same slow steady drift of days. He needs to see how lucky he is to have it. He needs to see what he's going to do with the rest of his life.

I need it too. I've missed the farm so much. But I want things to change as well. I want to get to know the sheep a little better; I want to be nicer to Priscilla too. Because it *can't* be the same as it was. The world is changing, all the time, and you have to change with it. You have to use what you have to make it better, even more special, even more beautiful than it already is. You have to plant small nothings while you can, as many as possible.

And there's no one else I would rather do it with. He is Tom, and I am Rebel. We chose each other.

The hill crests, and the road heads down to the farm gate that I've never once walked through. And that's the way that I get back home.

ACKNOWLEDGEMENTS

Thanks to (in chronological order):

Denise, for the idea;

Helen, for making me do it;

Jules, for being my Jaxon;

Katya, for the relentless support;

Annalie, for being the best;

Claire, for always fighting my corner;

Megan, for your diligence;

Laurissa, for having the patience of a saint;

Keith, for the amazing cover.

But more than anyone, thanks to Monty Richmond. You never once told me off for stealing your voice, because you're generosity incarnate and a tireless patron of the arts. But, also, because you're a dog.

"An enthralling, Narnia-flavoured novel."
The Guardian

Evacuee Col's sister is in grave danger. Together with
his guardians – a six-foot tiger, a badger in a waistcoat
and a miniature knight – he must race to Blitz-bombed
London to save her. But soon Col is pursued by the
terrifying Midwinter King, who is determined to bring
an eternal darkness down over everything.

"A story of hope and love."
Daily Mail

"[A] whirlwind adventure."
The Daily Telegraph

When an evil faerie steals Yanni's baby
sister, Yanni and his cousin, Amy, must
travel to goblin palaces and battle-swept
oceans to get her back. But faeries delight
in tricks and Yanni will need every drop of
courage, and even a few tricks of his own, if
he's to outwit the faerie and save his sister…

"Richly imaginative."
The Week Junior

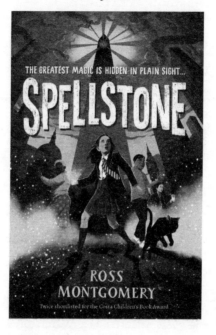

Evie is used to being overlooked – until she is
recruited into a secret magical organization, and
discovers that being unremarkable might just be her
greatest strength. Evil is returning to the land, and
Evie is the only person who can stop it. But how
can she defeat the most dangerous magician in the
world, when she doesn't even know her own powers?

ROSS MONTGOMERY started writing stories as a teenager, when he should have been doing homework, and continued doing so at university. His debut novel, *Alex, the Dog and the Unopenable Door*, was nominated for the Costa Children's Book of the Year and the Branford Boase Award. It was also selected as one of *The Sunday Times*' "Top 100 Modern Children's Classics". His books have also been nominated for the CILIP Carnegie Award, while his picture book *Space Tortoise* was nominated for the Kate Greenaway Award and included in *The Guardian*'s Best New Children's Books of 2018. *The Midnight Guardians*, Ross's first novel with Walker Books, was selected as a Waterstones Children's Book of the Month and shortlisted for the Costa Children's Book of the Year Award. He lives in London with his wife and their cat, Fun Bobby.

#IAmRebel
@MossMontmomery
@WalkerBooksUK